The Thief

Nancy Rue

PUBLISHING
Colorado Springs, Colorado

THE THIEF
Copyright © 1996 by Nancy N. Rue
All rights reserved. International copyright secured.

Library of Congress Cataloging-in-Publication Data
Rue, Nancy N.
     The thief / Nancy Rue.
        p.   cm.— (Christian heritage series ; bk. 8)
        Summary: Eleven-year-old Thomas struggles to learn about right and wrong even as
his older brother engages in a setup to get the Loyalists run out of town.
        ISBN 1-56179-479-1
        [1. Brothers—Fiction. 2. United States—History—Revolution, 1775-1783—Fiction.
3. Christian life—Fiction.] I. Title. II. Series: Rue, Nancy N. Christian heritage series ;
bk. 8.
PZ7.R88515Set   1996
[Fic]—dc20   96-8551
                                                                                           CIP
                                                                                           AC

Published by Focus on the Family Publishing,
Colorado Springs, Colorado 80995
Distributed in the U.S.A. and Canada by Word Books, Dallas, Texas

This author is represented by the literary agency of Alive Communications, 1465 Kelly
Johnson Blvd., Suite 320, Colorado Springs, CO 80920.

This is a work of fiction, and any resemblance between the characters in this book and
real persons is coincidental.

Focus on the Family books are available at special quantity discounts when purchased in
bulk by corporations, organizations, churches, or groups. Special imprints, messages, or
excerpts can be produced to meet your needs. For more information, write: Special Sales,
Focus on the Family Publishing, 8605 Explorer Dr., Colorado Springs, CO 80920; or call
(719) 531-3400 and ask for the Special Sales Department.

Editor: Keith Wall
Cover Design: Bradley Lind
Cover Illustration: Cheri Bladholm

Printed in the United States of America

96 97 98 99 00/10 9 8 7 6 5 4 3 2 1

For Kristin Richardson,
who lives the faith she believes in

A Map of
Williamsburg
1780–81

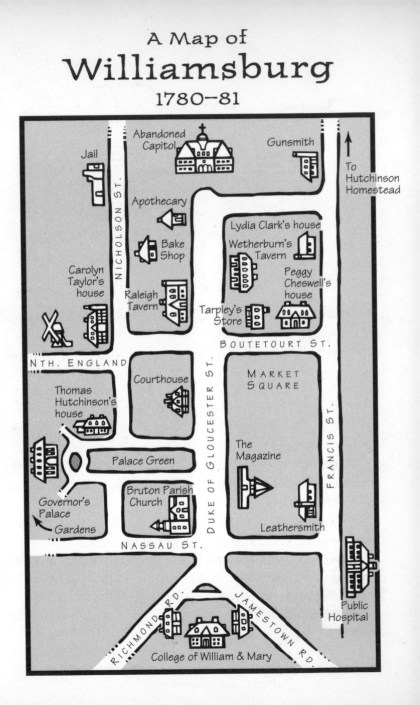

Chapter One

"**T**om Hutchinson! Are you using that tree to peek in my window?"

Like a big, floppy pup, Thomas Hutchinson groped for the branch above him, but his puppy-paw hands missed by an inch and he tumbled, black tousled head over silver-buckled shoes, to the carpet of grass below.

Caroline Taylor stood over him, hands on hips, shaking her sandy-colored hair.

"It serves you right," she said. "You were being a *Peeping* Tom up there, weren't you? Eleven years old—nearly 12—you should know better!"

"I wasn't *spying* on you," Thomas said, brushing the grass from his white linen sleeves. "I was hiding from you."

Caroline's smile, the one that reminded Thomas of a slice of melon, split open to reveal her shiny teeth—the ones that Thomas was sure were twice as big as his own.

Her brown eyes danced. "*Hiding* from me?" she said. "You would need a tree three times that size to hide, you big oaf!"

As Thomas stood up on his long log-legs, he folded his thick arms across his chest and then slid them down to his hips, looking for a place to rest them that didn't feel awkward. And then he grinned.

There were two things that only Caroline could get away with: calling him Tom and telling him he was a big, clumsy oaf. She was, after all, his best friend—even though he never got away with being anything but himself when she was around. And even though her parents were Loyalists and his were Patriots . . . and it was 1780 with a war going on between them.

"Esther's going to have you by the ear when she sees those grass stains on your shirt," Caroline said.

Thomas looked at them and groaned. "Forget Esther. What about Francis Pickering?"

"Are you on your way to work at the apothecary shop?" she asked.

Thomas nodded. "Why don't you walk me there?"

She twisted her mouth and fell into step beside him as they headed down Nicholson Street toward the back of Francis Pickering's Apothecary. As they moved slowly in the suffocating Virginia afternoon heat that hung on them like cobwebs, they seemed to be the only ones moving at all. Everyone and everything else seemed to have decided it was too hot to make the effort, from the ox standing like a statue on the lea beyond the jail to the black slave sleeping under a wagon in Elizabeth Tarpley's yard, his face all shiny with sweat.

The brick walls of Mistress Tarpley's garden soaked up the heat and threw it back at them, and Thomas wiped the tiny bubbles of perspiration off his own lip with his shirtsleeve.

"I was hoping we'd have time to play," Caroline said. "We've barely been to the Chinese Bridge at all since your father went off to Newport. Being the man of the house is taking up all your time."

Thomas grinned down at her again. "I didn't tell you. Papa's home!"

"When?"

"Last night. He docked at Yorktown yesterday and then rode all the way here to Williamsburg on horseback."

"Why didn't he stay at your plantation?" she asked. "Isn't it practically in Yorktown?"

"He's been gone a whole month. I guess he got anxious."

"Did he get plans for building warships?" Caroline said.

Thomas stopped and clapped his hand over her mouth. "*Shhh!*" he hissed to her as he glanced frantically over both shoulders. "There might be Loyalists listening!"

Caroline peeled his fingers off her lips. "I'm a Loyalist, ninny!"

"Your *father's* a Loyalist," Thomas corrected her.

When Thomas's father had told him it was all right for him to be friends with Caroline, Papa had said it was Caroline's parents who were Loyalists. He'd said she was still too young to have made up her mind whether she thought the King of England was right to try to keep the Americans from having their freedom, the way her father, Robert Taylor, and the rest of the Loyalist Tories did. Maybe, Papa had said, she'd end up believing in independence like the Patriot Hutchinsons.

"Well, did he get the plans?" Caroline said as they trailed on.

Thomas nodded proudly. "The people who build his

trading ships in Yorktown are going to start building ships for the war as soon as he gets back there."

They cut across the back yard of the Bake Shop, and Thomas sniffed the scent of shrewsbury cakes. "He's paid the way for another indentured servant to come from Scotland," Thomas said. "The man's supposed to be here any day. Papa says Esther and Otis are getting too old to do all the heavy work, especially with the horses." Thomas bunched his eyebrows together over his deep-set blue eyes. "I could do it, but Papa says I have enough to do working for old Francis and studying with Alexander."

"And playing with me," Caroline said. "Besides, you like those things. You do like having my brother as your tutor, don't you?"

They'd stopped at the steps that led up to the side door of the apothecary shop, and Thomas reached up to snatch a cluster of cherries off the tree. They were still yellow, but he popped two into his mouth at once and nodded at Caroline.

"Of course I do," he said with his mouth full. "He's a great teacher."

"You're going to get a stomachache, eating those."

Thomas stuffed the last two into his mouth. "If I do, I'll just get some spearmint from Francis—"

Just then the side door creaked open, and a wizened face poked out.

"Spearmint, eh?" it said in a voice like the wheeze before a cough. "I hired you to deliver my medicines, not take them yourself!"

Thomas swallowed the cherries whole and took the steps two at a time. He could hear Caroline tripping lightly up behind him and planting a noisy kiss on Francis's cheek.

"When will you teach this boy to get here on time, and with his mouth empty?" the old apothecary said. "And clean!"

"Don't be angry, sir," she said. "It's my fault he's late."

Francis's scowly face smoothed into a smile, and he patted Caroline's hand. "Then there must have been a good reason," he said.

He never fusses over me that way, Thomas thought, a little grumpily. But then, everyone fussed over Caroline. It took them a while to find out that Thomas was not as tough as he liked to appear, but they were drawn right away to Caroline like moths to a candle flame.

Old Francis hurried down the back hall, right by the steps that went down to the cellar and past his examination room into the main area in the front of the store. Even on his spindly bird-legs, he darted everywhere like a stiff old pigeon who always had something after him.

Caroline skipped along behind him, but Thomas immediately picked up his broom and began to sweep the hall.

Caroline came back to the hallway with a stick of cinnamon candy and sucked on it as she watched him.

"You really don't mind doing all this work every day?" she said.

Thomas shrugged. "I guess not."

"I would hate it. It makes me think of keeping house, and my mother says to me every day, 'You must learn to be a good wife.' Sometimes I wish I were a boy."

Thomas snorted. "I'd wish for something better than that if I were you. While I'm dusting bottles and delivering medicines, you're free to go and do whatever you please."

Caroline snorted back at him. "Don't try to fool me, Tom Hutchinson. You know you love every minute of it."

Thomas didn't say so, but that was actually true. When his father had first sent him to work for Francis last spring, it had been to shake him out of being a spoiled brat and a bully. Thomas remembered being madder than one of the hens when you chased her chicks—and being so terrified of old Francis that he'd thought if he made a mistake, the apothecary would turn him into a skeleton.

But as time had gone by, Thomas had learned everything about the shop and now knew most of the medicines Francis made here. After saving the old man's life one May afternoon, he'd felt better about being Thomas Hutchinson than he ever had before.

He stopped and leaned with a swagger on the broom. "I guess I am pretty good at it," he said to Caroline.

Suddenly, a shrill cry came from the front of the shop. "Hutchinson!"

Thomas dropped the broom with a clatter and tore around the corner. One foot flew out from under him, and he only barely managed to get his balance when he got to the counter. He could hear Caroline laughing softly behind him.

"Look alive, boy," Francis said. "There's someone here I want you to meet—if you can stay on your feet long enough."

Thomas noticed for the first time that there was a tall, willowy-looking man in the shop with eyes so pale they were hardly blue at all.

"Thomas Hutchinson, Dr. Nicholas Quincy," Francis wheezed. "Just arrived in town yesterday. About time we got us a doctor here, what with the rest of them going off to mend soldiers." Francis poked his hooked-over nose toward Dr. Quincy. "Tell the boy where you got your education."

Two patches of pastel color came at once to the doctor's white cheeks, and he ducked his head like a shy schoolboy.

Make that school girl, Thomas thought. This man didn't look like a doctor. He looked like a man who would make silly powdered wigs for giggly women.

"Well, I—" Dr. Quincy started to say.

"College of Philadelphia!" Francis cried, his head going red all the way to the top where his hair started. "The first doctor we've ever had in Williamsburg who actually went to medical school—and an *American* school at that. No England-trained physician, this one. He knows every one of the 21 medicinal plants native to our state." Francis took a raspy breath and pointed a long finger at Dr. Quincy, the way he often did at Thomas. "Tell him what you told me."

Nicholas Quincy ducked his head again as if he were embarrassed. The two pink spots on his cheeks turned crimson as he spoke softly. "I only said that the mild cures created from Virginia soil are less likely to interfere with the healing course of nature."

His lips went slowly into a wobbly smile, and Francis darted his beady black eyes at Thomas as if to see just how impressed he was.

Thomas said, "Oh."

He was still checking over the tall, thin man who, to hear Francis tell it, was going to perform medical miracles in Williamsburg. From the looks of him—long hands that looked like they'd never done a day's work and soft voice that had probably never stood up for itself—Thomas had his doubts. He

certainly wasn't like the strong men Thomas looked up to—
Papa, Alexander, his tutor, and Sam, his older brother.

"Come in, Mistress Caroline," Francis said. He waved
Caroline in from the doorway and presented her to Dr. Quincy
like she was the Queen herself.

It's easy to see why this doctor isn't out on the battlefield,
Thomas thought. *He wouldn't last a day at war.*

He'd heard his brother Sam talk about the fighting, how
tough it was, how brave you had to be, how much he wanted
to go.

Thomas shuddered. Every time that subject came up
when Papa was around, it ended with faces turning red and
doors slamming.

"It's a pleasure to meet you," Dr. Quincy was saying to
Caroline. He took the hand she offered him the way she'd
been taught, and he bowed slightly to her. Then he looked
around at no one in particular and said, "There's much to do
getting settled. I really must be going."

"I have to go, too," Caroline said. "I'll walk with you for a
ways."

Caroline beamed and the doctor gave the expected duck
of the head as he placed a small cocked hat atop his coffee-
colored hair and followed her to the door.

When it closed behind them, Francis was on Thomas like
a jay on a worm.

"That was a real doctor, Hutchinson!" he said, finger
pointing. "Not some dentist or barber, mind you! I'll thank
you to treat him with the respect he deserves!"

The swagger slipped out of Thomas's shoulders, and he
said meekly, "Yes, sir."

Thomas made it a habit never to argue with Francis when his spectacles were teetering on the bridge of his nose the way they were now. It was a sure sign that he wasn't fooling.

"Yes, sir," Thomas said again and turned to go back to his broom.

"And I suggest you befriend him," Francis said. "You're going to be working very closely with him."

Thomas whipped around and stared. "*I* am, sir?"

"We plan to combine our knowledge, Nicholas and I. If I send you out on a call with him, you will do exactly as he says, d'ya hear?"

"Yes, sir," Thomas mumbled. But as he retreated to the hallway and his broom, his thoughts were all shaking their heads.

Why can't I just work with Francis like I always have? He likes my work. I know what I'm doing here. Why does it have to change? That sissy doctor is probably a Loyalist, or even a spy. . . .

Thomas set his square jaw. He was feeling something familiar that he hadn't felt in a while—the first snapping sparks of anger.

But as he passed the afternoon reading labels for Francis and delivering ginseng to citizens of Williamsburg who were suffering from the heat, Thomas thought less about the doctor with the delicate hands and more about getting home to spend time with Papa. He'd been gone several weeks, and Thomas had a lot to report. His father had, after all, left him in charge when he'd gone to Newport, what with Thomas's oldest brother Clayton being out on their plantation taking care of things there, and Sam in school at the College of

William and Mary at the other end of town.

But as Thomas rounded the corner of the house that evening, his heart took a sharp dive.

The carriage was there from the plantation. Clayton was here, and since the horses had already been unhitched, he was probably staying at least for the night. That meant Clayton would take up all of Papa's time.

The sparks started to flicker in Thomas again, and he stomped off toward the water barrel behind the kitchen building to wash and cool down. It would be no good to go inside with anger plastered all over his face. Papa didn't stand for temper tantrums.

Thomas plunged his whole head into the water. It was lukewarm from the sun, but it was cooler than the thick air that would hang on until after sunset.

As he yanked his head out of the barrel and let the water fly out in all directions from his tousled curls, something caught Thomas's eye from the direction of the stables. Someone was going in—and he moved too quickly to be old Otis.

Thomas smeared the water from his face with his sleeve and crept toward the stable with his mind racing. Strangers had no business lurking around their horses. And with the war getting closer to Virginia, who was to say this wasn't a spy for the British, out to steal their animals?

Thomas plastered himself against the outside wall of the stable and listened. Then, barely daring to breathe, he leaned around the half-open doorway and peered in.

There, standing boldly as a liveried groom, was a thin, dark-haired boy, stripping the harness off one of the Hutchinsons' plantation horses. Anger burned up through Thomas like a brushfire, and he leaped inside the stable with his fists doubled.

"I've caught you, thief!" he cried. And with another leap, he was on the boy, pinning him to the ground.

⁜ ⁜ ⁜

Chapter Two

"I've got you, you lousy thief!" Thomas cried.

He pulled one hand away from the shoulder he was holding and clenched his fist for the first punch. With a heave of his body, the boy rolled to one side and grabbed Thomas's arm with a set of wiry fingers.

"I'm no thief, you fool!" he said. "Get off me, now."

His voice didn't sound angry, and his grip on Thomas's arm didn't tear into his flesh. But before Thomas could catch his breath, the skinny boy had him flat on his back and was holding him down by both shoulders.

For an instant, Thomas stared at him, frozen with surprise.

"There now," said the boy. "If I let you up, will you be leavin' me alone?"

The frozen moment passed in a flash of anger, and Thomas flopped like a fish to get out from under. The boy held tight, so Thomas brought up his knee and drove it into his thigh. The boy flinched long enough for Thomas to wriggle out and dive on top of him again.

"You *are* a thief!" Thomas shouted at him. "And I'll beat you to a bloody pulp for it!"

Thomas let fly with both fists. The boy caught him by one wrist and yanked him sideways. His face was turning red now, and his teeth were clenched.

"Let go of me, boy," he said to Thomas. "Or I'll be havin' to hurt you."

Thomas tried to push his hand into the boy's stomach, but he blocked him with his arm. His insides on fire, Thomas pounced on him.

And then everything happened at once. There was a scream from the doorway, and Thomas turned wildly to look. Something hard and fast crashed into his nose and knocked him backward. Sparks shot behind his eyes, but Thomas scrambled up to go for the boy again.

Then a hand closed over the back of his shirt and pulled him back. The boy got to his feet with terror on his face, looking at the person who was tugging Thomas's arms behind his back.

"He come after me," the boy said frantically. "I'm sorry. I was just tryin' to get him off!"

Thomas looked over his shoulder to see that it was old Otis, his father's servant, who was holding him back by his shirtsleeves.

Esther bustled stiffly over from the doorway and curled a gnarled hand around Thomas's ear. She was Otis's wife and had been Thomas's nanny since the day he was born—and Clayton's, and Sam's, and even his father's. Thomas winced as she squeezed tight.

"Is that true, Thomas Hutchinson?" she said. "Did you jump this boy?"

"I did!" Thomas cried, cringing. "But he was stealing one of our horses!"

"Stealing?" Esther said. She turned loose of Thomas's ear and cackled like a hen. "I don't think he'd be a-stealin' from the master the first day on the job."

Thomas stared at her.

"He's the new servant, ya simpleton! Malcolm Donaldson's his name."

Malcolm's dark eyes glimmered, and he said with a square smile, "Pleasure to meet you."

Of course, it made sense now. The thick Scottish accent, the black hair that appeared to have been lopped off with a butcher knife to make him look presentable, the telltale servant's clothing—brown shirt and coarse trousers made from striped mattress ticking.

But Thomas looked at Otis for confirmation. As always, the gray-whiskered old man only nodded.

"I suggest you do better at gettin' along with him in the future," Esther clucked. "It'll be up to you to show him how we do things around here."

Thomas could feel the resentment sizzling up his backbone. This was the second time today someone had told him who he had to be friends with. And he didn't argue with Esther any more than he'd pick a fight with Francis Pickering. She might be a servant, but she had been like a trusted member of the Hutchinson family since she was a little girl and had played with Thomas's grandfather, Daniel. And *her* father had worked for Great-Grandfather Josiah. Still, Thomas hated it when she told him what to do.

He smirked at Malcolm and pulled his sleeve across his

face to wipe off the sweat. The white linen he drew back was covered with blood.

"You've got yourself a bloody nose in the bargain," Esther said. "If I were you, I'd be a-washin' that off before I went in and faced your papa. You know how he feels about fightin'."

Thomas glared at her. Did she have to make him look like a baby in front of the first boy who had even been able to draw blood from him in a fight?

I'd have gotten the better of him if Esther hadn't peeled me off him, he thought angrily. *I'll have my chance to do it, too.*

As he stomped out of the stable, Thomas turned his head to shoot a warning glance at Malcolm. The servant boy was watching him, black eyes snapping.

His eyes are too close together, Thomas reassured himself. *He looks like a mongrel dog.* But his insides were shaky as he headed for the water barrel again. Malcolm didn't seem afraid of tangling with him again, though he was only Thomas's height and half his weight. Thomas dunked his head into the water, and the old anger he'd thought was long gone prickled stubbornly at the back of his neck.

Unlike his mood, the dining room was alive with merriment when Thomas entered. Candles flickered cheerfully up and down the mahogany table, and happy chatter rang from one end to the other. Side chairs were being scraped up, and creamware porcelain dishes were steaming with lobster, crab, and oysters.

But the only thing that brought a smile to Thomas's hardened face was the sight of Papa sitting at the head of the table, and Sam taking his place at his side.

"Sam!" Thomas cried.

Sam's tiny blue eyes twinkled as he grinned his confident grin across the room. Most of the time, there was no one Thomas would rather be like than his 16-year-old brother. But in looks, he knew he didn't have a chance. While Thomas's dark, unruly hair refused to stay back in a queue at the nape of his neck, Sam's blond curls were always tucked neatly into a tail that brushed his wide, square shoulders. Sam also moved with the sure gait of a deer, never tripping over his own feet as Thomas did now trying to get to him.

Sam gave the shout that always came before a burst of his laughter and squeezed Thomas's shoulder with a big hand. "Thomas!" he said. "Father, I think he grows more between every time I see him. He'll be bigger than both of us in a year."

Although Thomas was sure he could never be as big as his towering giant of a father, he felt himself turning red under the compliment and fumbled clumsily with the tablecloth as he sank into his chair. His 19-year-old brother Clayton sat next to him and passed his smooth gray eyes over Thomas.

"All that size won't do you much good if you never get control of it," he said. He tossed his powdered head, though not a hair moved from its slicked-back position.

Thomas glared at his china plate and refused to look up at Clayton's thin, know-it-all smile. *You're just jealous because you have those narrow shoulders and walk with a limp*, Thomas thought. *It's not my fault you have a weak heart and look pale and sickly all the time.*

But Sam's cheery voice broke in. "You'll catch up with those feet someday, Thomas."

"The hardest part is keeping him in clothes," Mama said.

Virginia Hutchinson sat at the other end of the table, smiling softly at her family. Each of her sons had inherited something from her—Clayton his big gray eyes, Thomas his dark hair, Sam his charming way—and it seemed to Thomas that she felt they were all part of her. She shook her head now until the ring of dark curls around her face bobbed and jiggled.

"It's bad enough that you grow out of them so quickly, Thomas," she said, "but do you have to tear them to shreds before that happens?"

Sam's eyes danced. "What does the other boy look like since you got through with him?"

Thomas followed everyone's gaze to his shirtsleeve, which was ripped open from cuff to elbow. He tucked the other, bloody sleeve under the table and looked quickly at his father.

John Hutchinson sat back in his chair at the head of the table, surveying his family with his deep-set, piercing blue eyes. The candlelight made his gold and silver hair glow, and for once the deep lines in his face were smoothed out with the pleasure of having his sons and his wife all together. Thomas didn't want to spoil that by bringing on The Look—the one where the bushy, dust-colored eyebrows knitted together, the mouth pressed into a stern line, and the eyes drilled into the victim with the anger that was brewing inside him.

"I was in the stable," Thomas blurted out, "with the new servant boy—"

"Ah, then you've met Malcolm," Papa said. "Though I'd hardly call him a boy. He's 15."

"When did he get here?" Sam said.

As Clayton went on to explain that young Donaldson had arrived in Newport on the ship *Mary Jones* a few days ago with his indenture papers all in order, Thomas shivered with relief. The conversation was steering away from the dangerous revelation that he'd been fighting with Malcolm.

"Well, just the same, Thomas," Mama said now, "give that shirt to Esther tonight so she can mend it."

Papa sighed. "There was a time when Esther would have used that one for scrubbing the floors, and we'd have simply ordered another one from England."

"I think those days are gone, Father," Sam said. "We're sure to be an independent country before long, and we'll have to produce our own goods."

Clayton groaned. "Before we get into any discussion that's going to give me indigestion, can we please pray for this food?"

"Please, do us the honor, Clayton," Papa said.

Clayton had graduated from the divinity school at the College of William and Mary and would be a minister of the Church of England right now if he could be ordained. But that would happen only if he went to England, since there were no bishops here in the colonies.

Clayton pulled out his copy of the *Book of Common Prayer* from his lavender waistcoat and flipped to a page with his lace cuffs ruffling. "'To our prayers, O Lord,'" he read stiffly, "'we join our unfeigned thanks for all Thy mercies: for our being, our reason, and all other endowments and faculties of soul and body—'"

Thomas's thoughts trailed off. He couldn't understand most of the words in the prayer book, and he felt a lot closer to God when he had his own conversations with Him.

Please, God, he prayed now, *make this food taste good*

even though Esther cooked it. And don't make me work with
Nicholas Quincy, and please don't make me be friends with
that conceited Malcolm Donaldson. And please, don't let there
be any arguments at the table.

His "amen" chimed in with Clayton's, and Papa began to
pile their plates high.

"We can thank Clayton for bringing this feast," Papa said.

"The Chesapeake Bay is teeming with seafood, as always,"
Clayton said.

"And it's a good thing," Sam said as he took a china
charger heaped with crab legs and Hutchinson garden
vegetables. "We won't be able to depend on imports anymore,
including the silks and satins and laces—all your bonnets and
gloves, Mother."

"We'll get along," Mama said—a little too cheerfully,
Thomas thought. She hated the arguments at the table, too.
"I'm already wearing last year's gowns, and I don't mind a bit."

Thomas looked at the pale-blue dress his mother was
wearing. The three-cornered cape around her shoulders
looked thin, but he didn't see what the fuss was all about. He
would wear the same clothes all the time if he didn't grow out
of them so fast. He cracked open an oyster and listened.

"But are you prepared to spin and weave that flax out
there when we have no more cloth made in Britain, Mother?"
Sam asked.

"I'll have you know," Mama said, "that just this week I
embroidered panels and sent them to the tailor to be made
into a vest for your father."

Sam shook his head. "Why, that's nothing compared to
the hardships that are coming—"

"Leave it," Papa said sharply.

There was an uncomfortable silence. Papa didn't like it when Sam wanted to talk about the war all the time. For a long time, Papa had refused to support it. He thought there must be a peaceful way for America to gain its independence. When the British had taken Charleston, South Carolina, last month, he had realized that the war was now very close and very real, and he was doing all he could to help. But conversations with Sam about it always ended up being battles themselves.

"So what do you know of the war, Father?" Sam said finally. "You must have heard something in Newport."

Papa sighed heavily. "I can see there will be no peace at this table until I get this out of the way. The British have a new commander in the South."

"What happened to General Clinton?" Sam demanded.

"He's gone back to New York with 4,500 of his troops."

"Well, that's good, isn't it?" Mama said. "Doesn't that mean there will be no more fighting in the South?"

"No, my dear," Papa said patiently. "Clinton claims that every man in South Carolina is either his prisoner or on his side now. But he still appointed a man named Charles Cornwallis to take over the army that's left down there."

"Clinton's a liar!" Sam cried. "There is still plenty of fighting spirit in South Carolina! I heard that our Continentals are moving down from North Carolina and that Baron de Kalb is in command of the whole lot of them."

Clayton sniffed. "De Kalb? Didn't he come from Europe with Lafayette? He's nothing but a soldier of fortune!"

"He was," Sam said. "But now he's as much a Patriot as I am!"

"That doesn't matter," Papa said. "Congress has replaced him with Horatio Gates—against General Washington's advice."

"With de Kalb in charge, we might have taken South Carolina back. The British are short on supplies, even horses. But I don't know about this Gates person." Sam leaned forward, both palms on the table.

Here it comes, Thomas thought miserably.

"Papa," Sam said. "I have to go down there and fight."

The Look formed on Papa's face as if it had been shot onto it with a musket. "Samuel, we have been through all of this before. I want you to finish school, set your*self* free, from ignorance—"

"There's barely a school left to finish!" Sam cried. "Most of the professors and half the students have gone. We can all finish when the war is over. I want to be a part of it now."

Papa's hand slapped down on the table and made the dishes clatter in their places. Thomas felt everyone at the table holding their breath.

"When will you leave off this romantic idea you have of war?" Papa said, leaning his face close to Sam's angry one. "I fought in the French and Indian War, son. It was cruel and it was bloody, as all wars are. I know what war can do—it's a very personal thing. It affects *people*, Sam, not just nations." His face softened a little. "In the North last month, I saw the soldiers marching barefoot in uniforms they'd pieced together out of bits of blanket and flour bags. I smelled the stench of hot, unwashed, sickly men—"

"I can take that, Father," Sam cut in, his chin set stubbornly. "I just have to do something."

"I didn't say you couldn't help," Papa said. "An appeal has gone out to all Patriots to donate every ounce of pewter and lead to be used to make ammunition. You can collect weights from clocks and window sashes—"

"That's not what I want! I want to fight!"

"No!"

The answer thundered out so loud that Thomas's spoon jumped on his plate. But it was the only thing that moved . . . until Sam pushed back his chair and bolted up from it.

"I would like to be excused, please," he said. His voice was cold, but his face burned with fury.

"Won't you be staying for Evening Prayer?" Mama said anxiously.

"No. I'm sorry, Mother. I have things to do."

Then he slashed across the room and out the door.

✢ ✢ ✢

Chapter Three

Although Mama tried to chat gaily about making bandages for the soldiers, the party feeling was gone from the table, and the Hutchinsons finished their meal in silence.

All through their family service of Evening Prayer in the parlor, Thomas tried to pray his own prayers over the voices of Papa and Clayton reading from the prayer book, but all he could really think about was Sam. His thoughts made him chew nervously at the inside of his mouth.

He won't do something stupid like run away and join the army without Papa's permission, will he? Even if he doesn't, will he ever come back? Will he ever speak to Papa again?

Thomas sighed. *Why couldn't it just stay like it was?* he thought miserably. *Why do things have to be different now?*

By the time Papa finished the last prayer with the words "be with us all evermore," Thomas was yawning and rubbing his eyes. But as he started to slip out into the front hall to go upstairs, Papa said, "Thomas, go out to the kitchen and help

Malcolm with the evening chores. It's late, and I'm sure Otis and Esther have already turned in. He will need some showing around."

Thomas wanted to shout, "No!"—but of course he didn't. He headed glumly for the kitchen building, where Malcolm was hunched at the table with a book and a lighted candle.

"Who said you could burn that?" Thomas asked.

Malcolm jumped and, seeing Thomas, glared intently. "No one," he said. "I thought it would be all right."

"Well, you thought wrong," Thomas said. He marched over to the table, licked his fingers, and snuffed out the candle with them. "There aren't enough for you to be wasting them."

Malcolm flopped the book closed and stood up. "Whatever you say," he said, his lip curled.

"Come on," Thomas said. "I'm supposed to show you what to do at night."

"I chopped the wood for the breakfast fire and fetched water from the well for tomorrow mornin'," Malcolm said as he followed Thomas out of the kitchen.

Thomas felt the hair on the back of his neck start to prickle. "I have to teach you about the horses."

"They're in for the evening, and I fixed that hinge on the top half of the stable door so it can stay open and they can get air durin' the night." Malcolm ran his wrist across his forehead. "It's sure hot here, even with the sun gone down."

Malcolm folded his arms comfortably across his chest as Thomas stopped and turned to look at him. It was as if Malcolm thought everything had been settled because he'd bloodied Thomas's nose.

Well, it isn't, Thomas thought fiercely. *And let's get one thing straight: You are the servant and I'm the master's son.*

"So, what else would you be havin' me do?" Malcolm said.

Thomas searched frantically through his brain. Malcolm had already done all the evening chores . . . and most of the morning ones, too. He could just hear Esther now, going on about how efficient Malcolm was—and what a clod Thomas was.

Thomas gritted his teeth. "You need to finish what you started with me earlier," he said.

Malcolm's dark eyes narrowed, and suddenly he looked much older than his 15 years. Close up like this, Thomas could see the faint traces of many fights on his face.

"What *I* started?" Malcolm questioned. "I'm thinkin' you've got that backward. It was you jumped on me, remember?"

"And it was you bloodied my nose," Thomas said.

To his surprise, Malcolm ran a nervous hand through his butchered hair and shrugged uneasily. "Sorry about that. I only meant to push you away when I caught you off guard, but—"

"You never caught me off guard!"

"Well, it's certain I did—when Esther came in and you looked up at her!"

"And if she hadn't," Thomas said fiercely, "I'd have bloodied your nose, and a lot more."

Malcolm stared at him for a long moment before he put up his hand as if to stop an oncoming stampede of horses.

"Look, Master Hutchinson," he said slowly. "I know I have to work for you as well as your father, and I'm tryin' to be civil about it. But you make it dreadful hard when you start hatin' me the first time you see me."

Thomas stepped forward with his fists clenched, but Malcolm didn't so much as flinch.

This is where you're supposed to back up and cower, Thomas wanted to say to him. *Don't you know the rules? Don't you know I've always been the bully?*

Until a few months ago, anyway. Then he'd stopped feeling so angry all the time, stopped wanting to fight everyone who crossed his path.

Why was it all coming back now?

But before Thomas could get an answer, a scream cut through the sodden night air. His head jerked toward the old Palace Green the Hutchinsons' house faced. "Where did that come from?" he said.

"That way," Malcolm said, and he bolted toward the street with Thomas on his heels.

Up and down the road on both sides of the Green, lanterns flickered on with alarm and doors slammed open as the sleepy citizens of Williamsburg stumbled out in their nightshifts. On one end of the Green, the deserted Governor's Palace stood empty and silent, but at the other, where the Duke of Gloucester Street met Bruton Parish Church, a wide figure in white stood howling.

Voices clattered against each other in the dark as the neighbors made their way down the Green.

"What on earth?"

"Who in the name of Beelzebub?"

"Has someone been killed?"

"Someone's died, you say?"

Thomas knew before he was within six feet of the woman that it was Mistress Wetherburn, the tavern owner's wife. She

came into the apothecary shop at least once a week and sent
her slave girl Cate in more often than that. Francis always said
there was no illness known to man that Mistress Wetherburn
hadn't imagined she'd had.

Right now it looked as if she had a case of hysteria. She
was standing on the corner in her nightshift and duster, eyes
bulging out of her very round face, her nightcap sitting
crooked on her head. Kneading her plump hands together
like a wad of dough, she was screaming, "They've stolen our
horse! They've stolen our horse!"

John Hutchinson reached her first and whipped off his
waistcoat to throw around her shoulders as he talked to her
in a soothing voice. "Your horse is missing, you say?"

"Not missing, *stolen!*" she shrieked. "Right out of the
stables. They've taken it!"

"Who?" said another voice from out of the gathering
crowd. "Was it one of those wretched Loyalists?"

Thomas took a step backward and only by sheer
willpower resisted the temptation to hide behind Malcolm.
The voice belonged to Xavier Wormeley, one of the magis-
trates of the court. No one hated Loyalists more than Xavier,
and because Thomas was friends with one, he hated Thomas,
too. It always paid to stay out of his sight.

"We didn't see who it was," said Mr. Wetherburn. He
arrived next to his wife, red-faced and out of breath. "Whoever
it was took one horse and had the other one untied. He must
have been frightened away when he heard me coming."

"That sounds like a coward Loyalist," Xavier said. His eyes,
which looked like holes poked into his pudgy face, scanned
the little crowd. "Don't you agree?" he said, jowls flapping.

"No, Xavier, I don't agree," John Hutchinson said. "Why must we assume at once that it was a Loyalist?"

Xavier looked at Thomas's father as he would at a five-year-old. "Because, Mr. Hutchinson, we all know that the British are in need of horses in South Carolina, and the only way the yellow-backed ninnies are going to win the war is to steal them from the Patriots!"

He looked around as if he expected a cheer to follow that statement, but the knot of people all looked at Papa.

"That may be true," Papa said. "But it's my job to watch the Loyalists in this town, among other things, and I don't know a single one who would stoop to stealing from his neighbors."

There was a general grumble of agreement, and the crowd began to splinter off toward their homes, sleepily calling out their sympathy to the Wetherburns over their shoulders. Cate hurried up in her nightclothes and threw a blanket around her mistress so that Papa could have his coat back, and the Wetherburns shuffled toward their house with Xavier behind them, waving his arms and jiggling his jowls.

"By morning, he'll have them convinced it was their own Loyalist kinsmen," Papa said. "Personally, I would bet it was a professional thief from New York rounding up steeds for General Clinton." He walked off toward the Hutchinson house with Clayton limping beside him.

"That was no professional," Malcolm said quietly.

Thomas looked at him sharply. "How do you know?"

"Someone who steals horses for his livelihood wouldn't be frightened off by the likes of those people."

"The Wetherburns," Thomas said.

"At least not before he got all he wanted. Whoever took their horse was new at this business." Malcolm yawned and added, "If there's nothin' else, I'll be turnin' in now."

"Go on, then," Thomas said. "But be up before dawn."

Malcolm's close-together eyes glittered. "Is that when you want me to wake you up?" Without waiting for an answer, he sauntered off toward the house.

Conceited know-it-all, Thomas muttered to himself.

A half hour before, Thomas had been ready to head for his own bed. But now he was wide awake, and the thought of going up to his steamy room and climbing in behind the mosquito netting was a smothering one. The night beckoned him up the Palace Green, past his house. A short walk might shake some of the confusion out of his head.

Everything looked so different than it had last night at this time, he thought as he crunched across the grass to the rhythm of the crickets chirping. The catalpa trees still lined the Green on both sides, and the peepers still called out from them, and the fireflies still pricked the darkness like flashing knife points.

But nothing else seemed the same. Last night he'd been the man of the house when Papa had come home, and his father had been so proud of him. He'd felt confident about his job at the apothecary, and he'd known no one else could take his place with old Francis. The whole summer had stretched out before him like a silky cloth, dotted with morning lessons done lazily in the dining room with Alexander, afternoons sticking his feet in the streams between deliveries, and evenings making up new games with Caroline to play behind the vacant Governor's Palace.

Now all he saw was himself following dull Dr. Quincy from house to house, listening to him drone on about his miracle cures. And then coming home to that swaggering little Scotsman and watching him do everything better than he himself could do it. And wondering every day if Sam was going to fight with their father forever.

With all of that, would there be any time to spend with Caroline in any of their favorite secret places?

Just then, the toe of his shoe caught on a rock, and Thomas tumbled headlong into the grass. As he rolled over to get his bearings, he chuckled to himself. He was there—in one of his and Caroline's secret places.

I must have been thinking so hard I didn't even know I was behind the Palace, he thought.

It was cooler here among the thick trees and the canal that ran through the gardens. Thomas breathed it in, and he could feel the hackles on the back of his neck starting to settle down.

It always felt good to be back here. He and Caroline had discovered it as the perfect play place last spring. The Palace and its gardens had once been the home of the British governors the King appointed to watch over the colony of Virginia. When the colonies had declared their independence four years before, in 1776, the *American* governors of Virginia had lived here, first Patrick Henry and then Thomas Jefferson.

Thomas hadn't lived in Williamsburg then. He'd grown up on the Hutchinsons' plantation near Yorktown. But Papa came here often in those days and had told him that Williamsburg had been an exciting place when it was the capital of Virginia. Thomas wished he could remember it that way, but since Governor Jefferson had moved the capital to Richmond, just before Papa had brought Mama and Thomas here, it was a sleepy town with nothing much going on except the College of William and Mary and the mill that Caroline's father owned.

But Thomas and Caroline had managed to dream up plenty of excitement here in the abandoned gardens. The Chinese Bridge over the canal was their best spot for becoming knights and warriors and villains in imaginary pointy helmets.

Thomas peered through the thick arch of trees that met over the canal and smiled to himself when the bridge took shape in the darkness. He could hear fish splashing in the water below it.

Maybe that's one thing that will stay the same, he thought as he hurried toward it. *The bridge, and Caroline, and us playing here at night after I leave the shop. Those rules don't ever have to change, because we make them.*

Sighing happily for the first time that day, Thomas put one foot up onto the bridge. Before he could take another step, a hand clapped over his mouth and snuffed out his breath.

✞ ✞ ✞

Chapter Four

For a moment, Thomas was paralyzed with terror. Someone was pinning his arms back. Someone was trying to suffocate him. Someone strong.

But then a voice whispered hoarsely in his ear. "It's me, Thomas. When I let you go, don't yell."

As soon as the big hand slid away, Thomas whirled around and cried out, "Sam!"

Sam grabbed his head and plastered his mouth shut again. "I told you not to yell, fool! *Shhh!*"

Thomas shook himself and looked over both shoulders into the darkness. "Why?" he whispered. "Why do we have to be quiet?"

Sam grinned down at him. "We don't want everybody in Williamsburg to know about this place, do we? We have to have somewhere to escape to."

"Who's going to hear me this late at night . . . ?" Thomas started to say. But his voice trailed off as he realized for the first time that Sam was soaking wet. "What happened to you?"

"I've just been for a little swim," Sam said. To prove it, he shook like a dog, spraying Thomas with cold canal water.

"Hey, don't get *me* wet!" Thomas cried.

"Why not? It'll cool you off! In fact, I think you should take a swim yourself!"

Before Thomas could protest, Sam grabbed him by both arms and shoved him, breeches, shoes, and all, into the canal.

Thomas plunged in with a splash and sputtered to the surface to find Sam paddling calmly in the water beside him.

"Feels fine, doesn't it?" he said, grinning.

"Feels better when you're all the way under!" Thomas shouted and hurled himself at his brother and dunked him beneath the surface.

Sam bobbed up, already lunging for Thomas's head and pulling him back under with him. Thomas squealed happily and grabbed a handful of blond hair on his way down.

They wrestled in the canal until Thomas cried "uncle" and Sam let him flop his way to the bank. Sam swam smoothly up to him and eased his muscular body out of the water with one arm. He offered the other one to Thomas.

"Can I trust you?" Thomas said.

"I'm your brother. Of course you can trust me!" Sam said—and then pushed his hand at Thomas's chest and shoved him back into the canal.

Thomas hooted as he pulled himself out. Sam stretched out on the grassy bank, and Thomas flopped down beside him.

"You've gotten stronger since the last time we wrestled, little brother," Sam said.

Thomas sucked in his cheeks and said in a proper voice, "But will I ever get this body under control?"

Sam gave his shout of a laugh. "Don't let Clayton bother you. It hurts him that he can't do the things we do, because of his heart and all. He wouldn't be so bitter if he could do what he's studied for all these years."

"You mean be a minister?" Thomas asked.

Sam nodded. "I think Papa should just let him go to England and take his chances. It would be better than being unhappy."

Thomas jammed his chin into his hands. "Anything would be better than being unhappy."

"What's this?" Sam's sandy eyebrows shot up like Papa's did. "Is there trouble in Thomas Hutchinson's world?"

"Yes," Thomas said.

Sam rolled over on his back and put his hands behind his head to look at him. "So, tell your big brother all about it."

Thomas hesitated only for a minute before he let it all fly out. "Well, first of all, there's a new doctor in town—and Sam, he's a sissy—and I have to work with him!"

Sam leaned up on one elbow and listened with his tiny blue eyes following every word seriously while Thomas told the whole story of Nicholas Quincy and Malcolm Donaldson and the way everything was suddenly changing.

"The only thing that hasn't changed is Caroline," Thomas finished.

Sam set his jaw. "So you decided not to listen to me when I told you how dangerous it is to keep company with a Loyalist's daughter."

"Caroline isn't dangerous, Sam!" Thomas said savagely. "I knew no one would understand—not even you!"

He started to get up, but Sam grabbed his arm. "Whoa

there, little brother. Now don't be so quick to judge."

Thomas looked at him doubtfully.

"Now," Sam said, "it sounds to me like you're pretty tired of other people running your life for you."

"Yes," Thomas said stubbornly.

"Who could understand better than I can? All I want to do is go off and fight for the cause I believe in, and my father wants me to stay here and act like a Quaker!"

"What's a Quaker?" Thomas asked.

"It's a religion. It's Christian, but it isn't Church of England. The people don't believe in war, and they'll do anything to keep the peace."

"So they won't go fight?"

"That's right." Sam's handsome face twisted. "But I'm no Quaker. I'm 16, nearly 17, and I think I should be allowed to join the militia or even the Continental Army if that's what I think is right." He smacked his hand against the grass. "I'm tired of doing what Father says. I know Clayton is. And now you are, too."

Thomas hitched his shoulders around uneasily. Sometimes Sam acted so much like a rebel, it was scary.

"Aren't we supposed to do what Papa says?" Thomas asked. "I mean, that's always been the rule."

Sam sat up straight and peered into Thomas's face. "What do you think this war is all about? They're out there fighting for freedom . . . independence. Everything is changing, Thomas. The old ideas—Father's ideas—are going to be run out with the British, you mark my words."

"What ideas?" Thomas said anxiously.

"The one that says 'a gentleman must have a sound

education in ancient classics and political theory,'" he said, sounding just like Papa. "And the idea that the son has to follow the path his father has chosen for him. Don't do it, Thomas. I'm not going to."

It seemed for a moment as if Sam had drifted off somewhere and forgotten Thomas was even there. Thomas watched him with his heart pounding.

More is changing than I even knew, he thought. *Will I know what to do if I don't listen to Papa?*

Suddenly, Sam got to his feet. "It's a beautiful southern summer night, Thomas Hutchinson," he said, his eyes twinkling again. "And here we are wasting it talking about serious things. Race you to the bend and back!"

He stepped to the bank and sliced into the water. Thomas dropped in after him like a cannonball and thrashed down the canal with all his might. He lost the race, of course. Sam was, after all, the best swimmer in Williamsburg . . . and maybe in all of the Tidewater cities, for all he knew.

By the time Sam walked Thomas home and slipped off into the darkness to his room at the College, the town was silent, and Thomas knew it must be past ten o'clock. Everyone in the house would be in bed by then, and he opened the back door like a cat, bare feet padding softly on the heart-pine floorboards, ears perked up for Esther lurking in the shadows, ready to grab his ear.

But the walls themselves seemed to be sleeping as Thomas shut the door behind him and tiptoed toward the stairs. He was almost breathing easily again when he reached the bottom step and heard voices coming from Papa's library down the back hall. Their snarling tone stopped Thomas in midstep.

"I cannot believe," Papa said, "that a young man who intends to become a minister can have so little faith."

To his surprise, Thomas heard Clayton laugh—a thin, brittle chuckle that crackled bitterly in the air.

"I've all but given up on that dream, Father. How am I ever to be ordained?"

"This war isn't going to last forever."

"It has already lasted four years longer than anyone thought it would. The chances of our bringing a bishop here now are no better than the chances of my running a race down the Duke of Gloucester Street. We have lost our power because our church bears England's name. The Church of England in Virginia is as crippled as I am!"

"You're wrong, Clayton," Papa said. Thomas was amazed that he sounded so calm. He'd half expected Clayton to be thrown from the library by his ear. "God will reward us. You must have faith."

Clayton slammed a hand down on the desk. It was an angry slap, and Clayton's voice matched it. "How am I to have faith when I see the Virginia militia in Yorktown waiting in terror for the arrival of British forces—and watch our plantation neighbors fleeing to Fredericksburg because they fear for their lives? I have no faith that this war is going to make anything right again!"

There was another silence, and then the library door was flung open and someone stomped into the hall with a halting step. Thomas scrambled to his feet and skittered up the stairs. He was safely in bed behind the mosquito netting before

Clayton could even begin to climb.

But even if Clayton didn't find him to shout at him, Thomas's own thoughts did.

Thomas tried to say his prayers, but the screaming thoughts just kept cawing in his mind like taunting crows.

Maybe nothing stays the same, they said. *Even God.*

✠ ✠ ✠

Chapter Five

Williamsburg summer morning always came early and noisily. Thomas opened his eyes and ears to it the next day and pulled the bedclothes over his head with a moan.

He'd stayed up far too late the night before to welcome the blue jays squawking in the garden, the crows cawing from the roof, and the sheep bleating right outside where a shepherdess was herding her fluffy flock out onto the Palace Green.

He would have gotten up and closed the window to shut it all out, but if he did that, his room would be as stiflingly hot as Esther's kitchen within minutes. Even at this early hour, Thomas could feel the perspiration forming in tiny beads under his nose.

It's going to be blistering doing chores this morning, he groaned to himself.

And then he shot up in bed and ripped off the covers.

Chores! He was supposed to teach Malcolm the morning routine!

He tore off his nightshift and replaced it with a cambric shirt and a pair of breeches, which he didn't bother to buckle below his knees. With his dark hair still standing on end from a night wrestling with his pillow, he tore past the stable, the chicken house, and the laundry to the kitchen building. In the doorway, he skidded to a stop and stared.

The breakfast fire was already burning merrily in the big brick fireplace, the rest of the day's wood was piled neatly next to it, and Malcolm sat at the cross-legged table sipping coffee and munching on a sugar muffin.

Beside him sat Caroline.

"Morning, sleepyhead," she said, grinning her slice-of-melon smile. "Malcolm and I were wondering if you were planning to get up at all today."

Thomas just looked at her as if his head were full of porridge. *"Malcolm and I?"* he thought dully. *What does she mean, "Malcolm and I?"*

Malcolm, he discovered then, was watching him like a hawk observing the chicken yard. "Esther made us sugar muffins this mornin' because the fire was ready so early," he said. He pushed a pewter plate stacked with them across the table. "Have one."

Thomas wanted to give him a cold, polite "No, thank you," but sugar muffins were his favorite, and they were one thing Esther could make that didn't taste like sawdust. He picked two and popped one into his mouth whole.

"Don't bother to introduce us," Caroline said, wrinkling her nose as Thomas chewed with bulging cheeks. "We took care of that ourselves."

I wasn't planning to, Thomas wanted to say, but his mouth was too stuffed.

Malcolm said, "And I think I have everythin' done. Except to make Esther a new rollin' pin. Have you seen the thing she's been usin'?" He leaned forward as if he had a long-held secret, and Caroline leaned with him. "No wonder her biscuits come out like boot leather, eh?" he whispered.

Caroline giggled. Thomas didn't. He swallowed a lump of muffin and said, "What are you doing here, Caroline? You don't usually drop by before breakfast."

"I've come with a message for you," she said. "Mama isn't well today, and she's going to need some of her medicine this afternoon. Will you tell Francis?"

Thomas nodded knowingly. Except for Xavier Wormeley, no one hated the Loyalists more than Francis Pickering. But ever since last spring, when Caroline's family had been so kind to him, he had taken it on as his personal duty to see after Betsy Taylor's poor health. Still, with Xavier Wormeley always poking about, Francis thought it best to keep that information secret.

Thomas looked harshly at Malcolm. "Don't breathe a word of this to anyone," he said.

Malcolm shook his head of badly cropped hair and stood up. "All secrets are safe with me," he said. "Now if you'll excuse me, I need to see Otis for a piece of pine."

"Well, well, Master Thomas," said a voice from the doorway. "It's about time you were a-gettin' up!"

Esther waddled in, hands on her enormous hips, shaking her mob cap with the gray curls peeking out. "Just because Malcolm here has arrived doesn't mean you're relieved of your duties."

Thomas bit the inside of his mouth to keep from barking back at her.

"My legs are a-painin' me this morning," Esther grumbled as she picked up a tray of dishes. "Here, boy," she said to Thomas. "You can set the table, since Malcolm has everything else done."

"Good day, all!" Caroline sang out. "I must get home!" And without a backward glance at Thomas, she sailed out the door with Malcolm behind her. The giggles Thomas heard outside the kitchen were muffled, but Thomas heard them, and his cheeks burned.

But when he reached the parlor where Papa always took his breakfast in the summer—so Mama could rest in the coolest part of the day—Thomas felt a chill that put out the fire in his face at once. It hung in the air between Papa and Clayton.

"Good morning, Thomas," Papa said stiffly.

Clayton just nodded at him and took a cup and saucer off the tray.

"There's sugar muffins," Thomas said lamely. "They're good—I mean, for Esther."

His father nodded, but Thomas knew he hadn't heard a word he'd said.

"So you'll be returning to the homestead today," Papa said in a voice Thomas was sure cooled his coffee.

"Yes," said Clayton. "I must see to breeding the cattle and upgrading the soil and improving the fruit trees . . . while I wait for my life to begin."

Papa slowly set his cup on its saucer. "I'll thank you not to be sarcastic with me, Clayton."

"Yes, *sir*," Clayton said. He stood up. "I really must be getting on."

Papa watched Clayton as he limped from the parlor, the tail of his yellow coat quivering behind him. Thomas watched Papa, and he was sure he'd never seen him look more sad.

"What does *sarcastic* mean?" Thomas said an hour later as he and Alexander sat in the dining room, preparing for the morning's lessons.

Alexander grinned his male version of Caroline's smile. He wasn't quite as blond as his younger sister, and he was certainly taller and looked more like a sportsman than she did, but their brown eyes, dimples, and big-toothed grins made them look almost like twins—seven years apart.

"It's when you say something you don't really mean."

"Then it's like lying," Thomas said. No wonder Papa didn't like it when Clayton did it.

"No," Alexander said, "because you say it in such a way that we know you don't mean it." Alexander's dimples deepened mischievously. "Suppose I were to give you a ciphering problem—such as, if to the double of a number, a second number be added, the half of the sum must necessarily consist of the said first number and half the second—and you said, 'Oh, Master Alexander, that's too easy. Give me a harder one,' I would *know* you didn't mean it. That's sarcasm."

Thomas gnawed at the inside of his mouth. "If you don't mean it, then why do you say it?"

"To be amusing," Alexander said. "Or to be, well, nasty."

"Oh," Thomas said. He was understanding it now. Clayton was saying he was excited to go back and run the plantation—instead of going to England to be ordained—but he wasn't. And Papa knew it.

"I suspect you've seen the nasty side of sarcasm this morning, young Hutchinson," Alexander said, looking at him closely.

"I have," Thomas said.

Alexander slammed his *Wingate's Arithmetic* book shut and leaned back in the mahogany side chair with his fingers laced on his chest. "I was looking for an excuse *not* to do ciphering. Talk."

That was all Thomas needed to hear.

"Is everything going to change because of the war?" he blurted out. "Are we all going to end up starving or becoming slaves?"

Alexander sucked in his dimples to think about it.

"You and I are not on the same side in this war," he said finally. "But I would never lie to you, you know that, don't you?"

Thomas nodded. Alexander might put a garter snake in his Greek grammar book or make him write an essay about chickens' lips just to practice his spelling, but he would never lie to him.

"All I know is, it doesn't look good for Virginia," Alexander went on. "Portsmouth is defenseless. Norfolk is in ruins. You see how naked Williamsburg looks. And Governor Jefferson has no one to protect us except the local militias, and I hear they run like rabbits every time they hear gunfire."

Alexander shook his head sadly. "The Patriots hope the French will come in and help them, but who did they have trying to convince the French? Lafayette! He was 18 years old! That's my age!"

Suddenly, a voice came from the doorway. "He may have been only 18, but he's good enough for George Washington!"

Alexander and Thomas both whipped their heads toward the door. Sam was standing there, blue eyes shooting a glare at Alexander like a ball from a musket.

Alexander stood up and extended his hand. "Sam!" he said. "It's a pleasure!"

But Sam ignored both the offer of a handshake and the greeting. He stepped to the table and leaned his hands on it, so that his nose almost touched Alexander's. Thomas swallowed hard as he saw the smile slip off his teacher's face.

"If you don't have the facts, don't talk to my brother, *Teacher*," Sam said. "Young Lafayette and General Washington have been friends since 1777. A unit from the Continental Army is this very minute in Richmond getting food and wagons and horses. We *will* win this war—no thanks to cowards like you."

Alexander's sunny face darkened. "How am I a coward?"

"You won't risk independence. You allow the British army to fight your battles for you, while you sit here in Williamsburg with my father protecting you. He ought to let Xavier Wormeley hang you like he's wanted to do since 1775!"

"Sam, no!" Thomas bolted up from his seat, knocking the chair to the rug behind him.

Sam narrowed his eyes suspiciously at Thomas. "Are you standing up for this . . . this Tory?" he said.

"No! Well, yes. I mean, he's not a Tory."

"Come now, Sam," Alexander said. "Why put the boy in the middle of this?"

Sam drilled his eyes into Alexander for a moment before he shot them back at Thomas. "He's right, you know," he said tightly. "You shouldn't be in the middle, Thomas, because you shouldn't be here at all. I've told you what was going to happen if you continued to keep company with the likes of him."

"He's my teacher!" Thomas cried.

"He's poison!"

"No!"

Sam put up his hand and stepped away. "All right, have it your way," he said through gritted teeth. "But I warn you, there will be nothing but trouble from it. He'll rub off on you like poison ivy."

With one last venom-filled look at Alexander, Sam turned and strode out of the room. Thomas felt as if he'd been kicked in the stomach. He clutched at his middle with his arms and charged for the window, where he looked out onto the garden until the tears backed out of his eyes.

"He's a liar," he said miserably.

"He's your brother, Thomas," Alexander said.

Thomas twisted to look at him. "Are you saying all of that was true?"

"In *his* mind, it's true."

Thomas dug his hands into his hair. "It's either true or it isn't!"

"I'm sorry, young Hutchinson," Alexander said sadly. "But when it comes to people's beliefs, that's the way it is."

✛ ✛ ✛

Chapter Six

*A*t least that's one good thing that's happened today, Thomas thought when he arrived at the apothecary shop that afternoon. *Dr. Quincy isn't here.*

"Hutchinson!" Francis squawked the minute he walked in the door. "Make yourself useful and bring me some comfrey roots from the cellar. Ulysses Digges has got himself cut open somehow, and they're calling for medicine at the college."

"Yes, sir," he called over his shoulder. "Oh . . . and sir?"

"What is it?" Francis said absently. He was back to hunching over his counter, eyes squinting at the powder he was measuring out.

"Mistress Betsy Taylor needs medicine today."

Francis nodded and kept squinting. "Comfrey, Hutchinson," he said.

As Thomas trotted down the stairs, he played his favorite guessing game—what was Francis going to do with the comfrey?

Probably boil it and make a poultice of it for the cut, he decided. It would be especially good to be right today, since

47

everything else was being turned upside down.

As he climbed the creaky staircase again with a fistful of comfrey, Thomas had another thought. Ulysses Digges was a good friend of Sam's at the college. He'd seen them hooting and shoving each other around after church on Sundays.

He's even bigger than Sam, Thomas thought. *Papa says he reminds him of a bull. If he got cut, it was sure it wasn't another boy did it to him.*

But the minute he cleared the doorway into the front shop, those thoughts evaporated happily. Mrs. Wetherburn's slave girl, Cate, was leaning on the counter, chattering to Francis in her high-pitched voice. She was always good for a few chuckles.

"Mistress done lost her mind sure this time," she was saying as Thomas put the comfrey roots on the counter. "Once that horse was stolen, she didn't sleep a wink, and you know who had to set up all night with her!" She rolled her enormous black eyes at Thomas, who grinned at her. She was probably in her 20s—older than Clayton—but she talked to Thomas like they ought to be climbing trees or throwing mud together.

"For the love of Saint Peter," Francis grumbled. "The woman's hysterical. I don't know what she'd do if her husband were stolen instead of a farm animal."

"Oh, mercy!" Cate cried, throwing her hands up to the bright-green scarf that was tied tightly around her woolly head. "Don't even suggest it, Master Francis! I'd rather be stolen away myself than have to nurse her back from those kinds of carryins-on!"

"She looked upset enough out on the street last night in

her nightclothes," Thomas said.

"You don't know nothin' 'bout it, Master Thomas!" she said. "No sooner had I got her into the bed, when she started chewin' on that nightdress!"

"Hutchinson!" Francis said sharply. "Quit your gossiping and check these bottles for me!"

Thomas scurried behind the counter, but he could see Francis's squinty eyes twinkling behind his spectacles.

He must be imagining Mistress Wetherburn eating her nightgown, just the way I am! he thought.

Thomas stifled a chuckle as he picked up the first black bottle and read its label to Francis. The old apothecary's mind was still sharp as a horsewhip, Papa always said. But only Thomas knew how badly Francis's eyes were failing. He depended on Thomas to make sure he wasn't putting the wrong ingredients into someone's medicine.

"Now you make a tea out of this feverfew," Francis said to Cate. "It's good for them that are giddy in the head. Should calm her right down. Meanwhile, you roast some onions under embers and mix them with honey, sugar, and oil. That will put her to sleep."

Thomas took the feverfew to the counter across the room to wrap it up. Cate leaned in toward Francis with her whole body fidgeting.

"They's one more thing, Master Francis," she said.

Old Francis scowled and said, "What is it now?"

"Mistress Wetherburn also say she'd like some sage for to whiten her teeth with, sir."

Francis stared so hard at Cate that Thomas thought he would bore holes through his spectacles.

"The woman is near to crazy because her horse has been stolen," he said finally, "but she can still worry about the whiteness of her teeth?"

Before she could answer, a voice rang out from across the room. "And well she might, because her horse will be recovered posthaste!"

They all turned to look at Xavier Wormeley, who had slipped into the shop unnoticed. In spite of the stifling Virginia heat, he was wearing his magistrate's cape, which he flipped about importantly as he crossed to Francis's counter. Thomas was sure he saw sweat dripping off the man's jowls.

Francis grunted. "It will, eh?"

"If I have anything to do with it, which I most certainly do." Xavier looked at Cate, who was gazing at him, open-mouthed. "What are you staring at, girl?" he said roughly. "Don't you know your place?"

Cate immediately shifted her eyes to the floor.

Thomas cleared his throat and beckoned to her with his head. She moved to his side of the shop, and Thomas pulled the sage jar off the shelf. He looked at Xavier and sneaked a grin at Cate. "It smells better over here anyway," he whispered to her.

"So what is it you've come for?" Francis said to the magistrate. "Marjoram for your ailin' stomach again?"

"It isn't medicine I've come for, Pickering!" Xavier cried, tossing his cape and sending the sweat beads flying. "I want information!"

Francis grunted again and pulled two white-and-blue jars off the shelf. "I have none of that," he said gruffly.

"But you're likely to hear some," Xavier shouted.

There really was no need to yell, Thomas thought. But then Xavier always spoke as if everyone else were 10 miles away.

"Everyone comes into this shop sooner or later!" Xavier said. "Someone may talk."

"I doubt anyone is going to walk in here and announce that he's stolen Mistress Wetherburn's horse!" Francis said.

"But someone might mention in passing that he's seen a Loyalist sneaking about, acting suspicious!"

Francis stopped pounding a powder with mortar and pestle and peered at Xavier, spectacles quivering. "Loyalist?" he said.

"Who else would steal a horse from a Patriot's barn?"

Francis shrugged and hunched over his powder. Thomas ducked behind the counter, pretending to look for newspaper to wrap Cate's packet of sage. Xavier was getting into dangerous territory.

"I know you don't treat nor sell to Loyalists," Xavier said. "And I'm glad of it. But if you hear anything at all about any dark dealings with them, you send for me at once, d'ya hear?"

Behind the counter, Thomas felt the old anger sizzling at the back of his neck. How dare Old Jiggly Jowls talk to Francis like that? He wasn't half the man the old apothecary was!

And then Thomas paused. Why was it so quiet in the shop? Xavier never left without making a grand exit, and he hadn't heard one.

A shadow fell over the counter, and Thomas looked up slowly. Xavier was leaning over, looking down at him from his poke-hole eyes.

"You, boy!" the magistrate cried. "Get up here. I want a word with you. Get up, I say—in the name of the law!"

Thomas rose and tried to keep his heart from pounding out of his chest. He'd had dealings with Xavier before . . . and they'd always led to more trouble than he could ever have imagined.

"What were you doing down there?" Xavier pressed.

"He is working for me, Wormeley," Francis barked at him. "I'll thank you to stick to your own business."

"Whatever this boy does is my business!" Xavier snarled back. "He's known to hang about with Loyalists, you know!" Xavier's tiny eyes grew even smaller as he drilled them into Thomas's face. "Did you learn your lesson last spring, boy? Or are you still keeping company with the likes of the Taylors?"

The shop grew as silent as the cemetery. There was no use trying to keep his heart from tearing out of his chest. It felt like it was already happening.

"In heaven's name, leave the boy alone!" Francis's voice wheezed. "If the boy sees anything suspicious, he'll report to you at once. I'll see to it."

The magistrate sniffed loudly. "I will hold you to that, Mr. Pickering," he said. "I know I can't count on his father to force him to. John Hutchinson calls himself a Patriot, but he's a Loyalist sympathizer himself. He may be a Loyalist spy for all I know!"

He's not! Thomas wanted to scream at him. *He protects the rights of the Loyalists to live in this town, but he's a Patriot through and through!*

Francis must have seen Thomas digging his fingers into the countertop, because he said quickly, "Boy, wrap this horseheal syrup and then deliver it."

Thomas didn't have to be asked twice. He crouched

behind the counter with the vial and his newspapers until he heard Xavier say "harrumph" and puff his way out of the shop. Even then, he looked cautiously over the top of the counter before standing up.

"I best get this medicine to Mistress Wetherburn," Cate said. But she stopped at the door and surveyed the street before stepping outside. Thomas thought her black face had gone a little pale. "He's the work of the devil hisself, he is," she mumbled as she crept outside.

Thomas held out the package of horseheal syrup. "Is this for Mistress—?"

"Yes!" Francis hissed at him. "And you deliver it same as always. No man—magistrate or king!—is going to tell me who I may bring to health!"

Francis's entire head was red, and his spectacles quivered as if his nose were an earthquake. Thomas hurried for the door, his heart still pounding.

"Hutchinson!" Francis said when Thomas's hand was on the doorknob. "Take a roundabout route, eh?"

Thomas knew what he meant, and he knew where he was going with the syrup. Horseheal, ground into a powder and mixed with sugar and boiled apple, was for breathing problems. The only person in Williamsburg Francis had ever mixed it for that Thomas knew of was Caroline's mother, Betsy Taylor. And taking a roundabout route meant making sure that Xavier Wormeley didn't see him.

The air was heavy with heat as Thomas made his way up the mile-long Duke of Gloucester Street that cut through the center of town. Even the flag hung limply on its staff at the post office, as if it were waiting for a rescuing breeze.

It was the new flag, bright with its red and white stripes and its blue field of 13 stars, and Papa had told him it stood for freedom. But Thomas felt as frightened as any slave must as he hurried around the corner at the Prentis Store and tried not to look over his shoulder.

Even more rules are changing, his jumbled thoughts said. *Now Francis is telling me to disobey the magistrate!*

But Thomas's mind paused. Actually, that didn't feel so bad. Xavier was a mean, cold, sniveling man who went to church only to be seen sitting in his honored pew up front. Maybe some rules changed for the better.

Thomas smiled to himself as he hopped behind Mistress Tarpley's garden wall to get away from the dust set up by a passing carriage—and the possible spying eyes of Xavier Wormeley. No one worked the gardens in the heat of the afternoon, and he could slip unseen all the way to Nicholson Street and right up to the side door of Caroline's house, where her father's study was. Having permission to say a silent "no" to Xavier was almost as good as going to Caroline's cheerful house, and right now he was doing both.

But when he put his hand on the picket gate, he saw Xavier Wormeley across the street, knocking at Caroline's door.

✝ ✛ ✝

Chapter Seven

homas coiled behind the gate and peeked through its slats. Xavier was whisking his cape around, knocking impatiently, and Thomas's heart started to slam against his chest again.

How will I get this in to Mistress Betsy with him there? he thought. *Maybe the Taylors will see who it is through the window and won't answer.*

But the shiny black front door swung open, and Thomas could see Alexander in the doorway. Xavier nearly shoved him backward as he swept past him. Thomas's heart sank as the door sighed shut.

Francis would holler for sure if Xavier Wormeley found out he was having medicine delivered to Mistress Betsy. Worse than that, Xavier would never give Francis a moment's peace if he knew.

I'll go back to the shop, Thomas thought. *Francis will know what to do.*

He was about to turn around and go back through Mistress Tarpley's garden the way he came in when something bright-yellow fluttered out of one of the upstairs windows in the Taylors' house. Squeezing his eyes to see, Thomas realized it was Caroline, and as he watched, she leaned out even farther until everything but her legs was hanging out the window. He raised his hand just high enough to wave.

Her face broke open into her slice of a smile.

"*Pssst!*" she hissed into the sodden air. "Back door!"

Thomas nodded and then crouched down again. He scanned the bottom story to Robert Taylor's study. The only thing he could see was a large black form pressed against the glass—Xavier Wormeley leaning on the window.

Opening the gate only wide enough to squeeze through, Thomas wiggled out of Elizabeth Tarpley's garden and skidded across the road like a dog with its head low and its tail tucked between its legs. As he cornered the house and met Caroline at the back door, he panted like a dog, too.

Caroline's brown eyes sparkled with excitement as she let him into the dark rear hall and up the narrow back staircase.

"This is an adventure!" she whispered to him when they reached the second floor.

"You wouldn't say that if you'd been the one hiding from Xavier Wormeley out there in somebody's arbor!"

Caroline looked at him sideways. "Yes, I would."

Thomas had to nod. She probably would.

They tiptoed down the hall past the wide front staircase and Caroline stopped for a moment to listen. They couldn't hear what was being said behind the study door, but they could pick out the voices.

Alexander's bright, excited chatter.

Robert's calm, serious tone.

Xavier's shout.

"He sounds as if he were at a wrestling match," Caroline whispered in disgust.

Thomas gave her an uneasy push. "Let's get into your mother's room before he comes out and sees me," he whispered back.

Caroline shook her head as he followed her toward the bedroom. "For someone who used to be a bully, you have no sense of adventure, Thomas Hutchinson."

Betsy Taylor's room was a place Thomas always loved to be. She always looked up from her pillow out of a face surrounded by miles of golden hair and smiled as if she'd been waiting all her life for him to walk in the door.

"Thomas, how wonderful to see you!" she said.

Thomas shrugged and mumbled "thank you," but he felt warm as he handed her the neatly wrapped package of horseheal.

"Is this my usual?" she said, and then fell into a fit of coughing that sent Caroline hurrying to pour a drink from the square posset pot on the bedside table.

Thomas had never heard her cough quite that hard, and he chewed nervously at the inside of his mouth. But she finally caught her breath and smiled at him again.

"I don't suppose you have time for a game," she said.

Thomas shook his head. He had spent a number of evenings in this very room with Caroline and her mother playing board games with wax figures and spinning totems, and although he always seemed to lose, he loved to play. "I have to get back to work," he said. "You know old Francis."

"Indeed, I do," Betsy said, pale face glowing. "But he

has a soul as sweet as an angel's."

Thomas wasn't sure about that, but he nodded and grinned a good-bye. Once they were out in the hall, Caroline grabbed his arm and charged toward the stairs with him in tow.

"You do have time to help me find out what they're talking about down there," she murmured to him.

"Caroline, no!"

"*Shhh!*"

"I can't let Xavier catch me!"

"He won't catch you. I have a plan."

Thomas tried to pull away, but by then they were at the bottom of the back staircase, and Caroline was yanking him into a dark corner just outside a closed door. This, Thomas knew, was the rear entrance to Robert Taylor's study, where he carried on the business of owning and running the mill behind their house. Caroline pointed to the door, silently clapped her hands, and then put her finger to her lips. Thomas sighed and pressed his ear against the door as she was doing.

This is probably against some rule, Thomas thought. *But they're changing so fast, I can't keep up with them anyway.*

"We have been through all of this before, Mr. Wormeley," Robert Taylor was saying in his low, patient voice. "It has always been agreed in this town that if a Loyalist keeps to himself, pays his taxes, and does not spy or enlist in raids against the Patriots, he will be allowed to remain in his home and conduct his business. I have done all of that. Why must you come here and threaten me?"

"Because I believe that he who is not for us is against us," Xavier blared out. "Neither you nor your son has enlisted in the militia—"

"I was excused from that even before the war started," Caroline's father said. "The law states that the miller is too important to the life of the community to leave it to serve in the army. Who would replace me? And without a replacement, how would you have your grain ground for flour?"

"There is a law proposed in Richmond this very minute to erase that evil rule!" Xavier cried.

Here we go again—changing the rules, Thomas thought.

"Until that happens, I believe I am well within my rights to live my life peacefully here without being constantly accused of wrongdoing by you, sir," Robert Taylor said. The patience was quickly draining out of his voice.

"How do I know you aren't aiding the British cause in secret? Where were you last night, just after dark?" Xavier asked.

Thomas could almost see him poking one of his sausage-like fingers.

"I?" they heard Alexander say. "Right here in our parlor, listening to my sister play the piano-forte."

"And you?"

"I have told you, Mr. Wormeley, I was here with my family. Neither I, nor my son, nor any of my Loyalist friends has stolen Mr. Wetherburn's horse, I assure you."

"I must see your stables, sir," Xavier said.

His demand was like a cannonball shot through the study.

"You may do nothing of the kind!" Robert Taylor cried.

"I do not need your permission—"

"But you'll need John Hutchinson's! He is responsible for protecting the rights of the Loyalists in Williamsburg. I'm sure he would not have you searching my property as if I were a common horse thief!"

"Your unwillingness to allow me to prove your innocence is evidence of your guilt."

Thomas heard a wet sound, as if the magistrate were smacking his thick lips. Thomas shuddered. Beside him, Caroline did, too. Thomas looked down at her and, in the dark of the tiny corner, saw something glistening on her cheeks.

"Alexander," Mr. Taylor said from inside the study, "go and fetch John Hutchinson."

"There is no need to do that," Xavier said quickly. "I shall be on my way. But I warn you both—I shall be watching you. You have not convinced me that you are not stealing horses to give to the British in South Carolina. And if I find out that you have, only God will have mercy on you."

Somehow the word *God* didn't sound right coming out of Xavier's mouth. Thomas leaned down to tell that to Caroline, but she was wiping at the tears on her face with two pink fists.

"My father is not a thief!" she hissed to Thomas. "He's not!" And with that she squirmed from the corner and disappeared down the hall.

I've never seen her cry before, Thomas thought as he made his way back to the apothecary shop. *She's always smiling or saying there's a way to fix it. She never gives up.*

A wave of sadness swept over him . . . and he never liked sadness. It was much easier to get angry.

Who is Xavier Wormeley to push his fat way in and accuse people who haven't done anything wrong? he thought savagely. *He's nothing but an overgrown sausage with saggy cheeks!*

Now, that felt better.

✢ ⚜ ✢

Chapter Eight

A s long and scorching as the day had been—and as many times as Thomas had peeled his sweaty shirt away from his skin—the night was falling cool and sweet and all-of-a-sudden as Thomas walked home that evening.

The peepers were starting their twilight chorus in the mulberry and catalpa trees, and a few fireflies had already started winking above the box hedges. Thomas lunged to catch one between his hands just as something silky slipped between his legs. He fell headlong onto the stone sidewalk.

"Thomas, are you all right?" Caroline leaned over him as he groaned and held his elbow. "You tripped over Martha, you silly goose."

Thomas moaned. "Better to trip over her than have her attack me."

Martha was Caroline's fat orange cat, who would just as soon scratch a person's eyes out as look at them—unless it was Caroline, of course. There wasn't a soul on earth, man or beast, who didn't love Caroline.

Thomas rolled over, still holding his elbow and groaning. But the minute he saw Caroline's face, he forgot everything else.

Her brown eyes were puffy and red, and her cheeks were covered with angry-looking blotches. She must have been crying ever since that afternoon, Thomas decided.

He gathered himself up off the sidewalk and stood up. He looked down at her arms dangling like wilted sunflowers at his sides.

"What's wrong?" he asked.

Caroline poked her toe at a weed that was straining to come up between the stones in the sidewalk. "Xavier Wormeley came back to our house after you left to tell us that another horse was stolen—this time from the leathersmith. Xavier wanted to talk to Papa or Alexander, but they were both gone from the house." Her eyes filled with tears again, and her voice grew shaky. "He said . . . he said they were probably out finding a hiding place for the leathersmith's horse!"

Her face broke, and she buried it in her hands as she sobbed—big, tearing sobs that ripped right through Thomas.

"Don't cry, Caroline," he said—because he couldn't think of anything else to say.

"Why not? There's nothing else to be done." She shook her head, still smothered in her palms. "Xavier Wormeley will surely find a way to place the blame on Alexander and my father. You know how he hates them for being Loyalists!"

Thomas folded his arms across his chest, then ran them down the sides of his breeches, finally planting them on his hips. Caroline was crying quietly now, but she was still crying. Thomas poked her shoulder.

"Come on, then," he said. "We'll go see what my father has to say about it. He can help. I know it."

Caroline shrugged—*as if she's given up*, Thomas thought. He walked uneasily beside her toward his house. Caroline Taylor never gave up.

When they reached the yard, just outside the Hutchinsons' stable, Caroline stopped and clawed at his sleeve.

"Thomas," she said. "I just thought of something!"

"What?"

"Horse thievery. They punish that by hanging people!"

She burst into a new round of tears, and Thomas looked at her helplessly. What could he say? That was the truth. With horses being used for transportation and planting and pulling loads, a family could hardly live without them.

"What have we here?"

Thomas looked up to see Malcolm coming toward them, peering closely at Caroline.

None of your business, certainly! Thomas wanted to say.

But Caroline looked up at Malcolm with her face streaming. "They're going to kill my father!" she cried.

Malcolm stared from one of them to the other.

"They're not going to kill your father!" Thomas said. "I mean, at least not yet . . . at least not unless they find out . . . I mean . . . "

Caroline blinked at him, and then wailed louder than ever. Malcolm looked as if he were fighting back one of his square smiles.

"I don't think that quite did the trick, Thomas, my boy!" he said. "Do you want to come in the barn and try to sort things out, lassie?"

Thomas shook his head, but Caroline—the lassie—nodded hers and followed Malcolm into the stable. Thomas could feel his neck starting to burn.

Caroline settled herself on a pile of hay, and Malcolm clucked softly to Judge, Papa's bay, as he picked up a leather harness and began to rub grease into it. Thomas slumped against a stall and scowled at them both. Musket, Otis's old bag-of-bones horse, watched him from the next stall with bored eyes. Burgess, Judge's brother, nuzzled him from behind. Thomas brushed his nose away angrily.

Caroline poured out her story to Malcolm. When she was finished, Malcolm narrowed his eyes at her.

"So what will you be doin' about it?" he asked.

Caroline's sandy eyebrows went up. "Do? There's nothing I can do! Thomas's papa and old Francis are the only people in Williamsburg who believe in us anymore. Xavier has turned everyone else against us!"

"All the more reason for you to be gettin' in there and fightin'," Malcolm said.

Thomas snorted. "Fight? How is *she* going to fight Xavier Wormeley?" He didn't add that *he* hadn't had much luck plowing into him.

But Caroline was cocking her head at Malcolm, and for the moment the tears had stopped falling. "Just how would I do that?"

Before he could answer, a long shadow fell from the stable door, and Otis cleared his throat at them.

"Yes, sir?" Malcolm said.

"Master needs his horse in a quarter of an hour."

Malcolm sprang to his feet and said, "Yes, sir!" But Otis

was gone without another word.

Caroline stared after him. "That's the most I've ever heard him say!"

"See that, lassie, you've cheered up already!" Malcolm said to her. "Hope will do that for you, you know."

"What hope?" Thomas growled at him.

Malcolm opened the stall and gently coaxed Judge out. "Hope for her father," he answered. "As soon as I have this horse ready for Master Hutchinson, perhaps I can be of some help in figurin' somethin' out."

He reached for a currycomb, but Thomas got there first— with a fair amount of stumbling—and snatched it up. Judge whinnied softly and did a sidestep.

"Whoa, there," Malcolm said evenly, soothing the horse. He curled his lip at Thomas. "What would you be doin' with that?"

"It's my father's horse," Thomas said. "I can groom him for the ride."

Malcolm looked him square in the eye for a moment and then backed away with a phony bow. "Very well, sir," he said. He picked up the harness again and continued to rub, even though it was already glistening in the near-darkness.

Thomas went at Judge's shanks like he was scrubbing a floor. He wasn't sure why he'd volunteered to do this. He'd only helped Otis with it a few times while Papa was away. It was just that he felt the same way about Malcolm touching their horses as he did about him being the one to cheer up Caroline. Angry.

"You'll be drawin' blood in a minute," Malcolm said mildly.

"I know what I'm doing," Thomas said.

Malcolm shrugged and turned to Caroline. "It seems to me, lassie, that the thing to do is find out who *is* stealin' the horses. Then that fat magistrate couldn't possibly be accusin' your father and your brother any longer."

"How did you know he was fat?" Caroline asked.

"He come here today, too. He was out in the yard, howlin' at Master Hutchinson about how the Loyalists were robbin' everybody blind." Malcolm chuckled. "He even asked him where I was during the stealin'!"

"You?" Caroline said, wide-eyed.

Is that so surprising? Thomas thought. He gave a long swipe of the comb and looked suspiciously at Malcolm. The comb did a flip-flop and slipped out of his hand onto the stable floor. Judge nickered nervously and tossed his head. Malcolm scooped up the currycomb before Thomas could even lean over.

"Here, let me show you the proper way—lad," he said, square mouth twisted into a smirk.

"No!" Thomas shouted. "I know how!"

He lunged for the comb, but Malcolm was already stroking it through Judge's tail with an expert wrist.

"Let me have it!" Thomas cried.

"Thomas, don't be a ninny!" Caroline shouted over him.

"Here, here! What is this nonsense?"

Everyone's voice froze as John Hutchinson strode into the stable. Thomas backed away from Malcolm, his chest heaving.

"Nothin', sir!" Malcolm said brightly. "Just a lively discussion is all!"

Papa scanned the stable with his riveting blue eyes,

stopping only to nod politely to Caroline. "Is Judge ready yet?" he said finally.

"Almost," Malcolm said as he slid the harness on. His hands worked with such speed that even Papa seemed hypnotized by them. "I'm a little slow still, this bein' only my second day and all."

Papa's deep laugh rumbled through the stable. "Slow? My boy, I couldn't be as deft as you are on my best day!"

Malcolm gave a respectful smile. Thomas clenched his fists. *You're nothing but a show-off, Malcolm Donaldson!* he thought. *But I'll show off for you one of these days!*

Just then his eyes met Caroline's, and he couldn't stop himself from gulping. She looked as if she knew exactly what he was thinking.

"Thomas, get yourself cleaned up for Evening Prayer," Papa said. "Then I must be off again."

Thomas marched obediently out of the stable, but not before he shot a parting glance at Malcolm. He tried to make his eyes threatening. Malcolm looked back and smiled his square smile.

Why did Malcolm have to come here and start impressing everyone? Thomas thought later, when he had climbed into bed.

Another thought was, *Why does Caroline listen to him? She doesn't even know him!*

Why does Xavier Wormeley get to be the boss when he's so mean? Why is he so mean when he's supposed to be on the Patriots' side?

Who's stealing the horses if it isn't the Loyalists?

Is *it the Loyalists?*

Thomas stared up at the hook in the ceiling that held the mosquito netting. Caroline and Alexander and even Betsy Taylor were his friends. Robert Taylor had helped Papa out of a pile of trouble last spring. It was impossible to think that they would be involved in stealing horses.

Then why was he thinking it? Because Robert and Alexander had been away from home when the leathersmith's horse was stolen? Because Robert Taylor wouldn't let Xavier look in his stables? Because no one else in town had a reason to take valuable animals from Patriots?

The only person who could answer questions like that was Papa, but right after supper he'd galloped off to Richmond to do his work for the war effort. Thomas sighed and squeezed his eyes shut. Not only were the rules changing, but there was no one to explain it all to him.

✝ ✦ ✝

Chapter Nine

𝔄 nyone passing through Williamsburg the next week would have thought it was a sweet, sleepy little town taking its rest under the broiling Virginia heat.

The cherries turned red, and the squirrels had a feast on them.

The apricots came in rock-hard with velvet skins, and the yellow plums in the little orchard across the street from the church begged to be picked—and were.

It might have made the casual traveler think of the Garden of Eden.

But nothing could have been further from the truth.

Mistress Tarpley, the Prentis family, and the Reverend Edmond Pendleton all had their horses stolen. Thomas watched the circles under Caroline's brown eyes grow darker each time Xavier Wormeley stormed up to the Taylors' front door demanding to know where Robert and Alexander were at the time of the theft.

"I'll catch them yet!" he cried to a small crowd in front of the Raleigh Tavern one afternoon. Thomas wanted to hurl a rock at him . . . but didn't.

There was also word from South Carolina that General Gates needed more men for the attack he was planning.

The shepherdess was run off the Palace Green so the straggly Williamsburg militiamen in their homespun civilian clothes could drill there at sunset. They would come up the street and wheel toward the Green, and when their major commanded "Present—give fire!" barking muskets clouded the air with black-powder smoke.

Sam shook his head as he gazed out the parlor window one evening when he was visiting Thomas and his mother.

"That 'major' used to be the bully boy of the grammar school," he said. "He can scare those yokels into obeying him, but he'll be worthless in battle." Sam gave a disgusted sniff. "Besides, if those are the 'troops' Thomas Jefferson is sending to Carolina, we might as well all start packing our things for prison. Most of those men are shooting old-fashioned hunting pieces, not military weapons!"

He turned to Thomas, eyes glowing. "I've heard tell of a group of American fighters in the swamps down in South Carolina who are giving the British a run for their money. They don't stand in lines shoulder to shoulder and fire like that show out there, mind you. They slip around in the marshes— the land where they grew up—and sneak up on those Redcoats from behind." He squeezed Thomas's shoulder with his big hand. "That's the kind of fighting I want to do."

"Please, Samuel," Mama said from her chair by the window. She set down the old shirt she was mending for a soldier to wear, and her shoulders sagged. "You know how upset we get when you talk that way."

Sam crouched down beside her and took her hands in his. "Papa gets upset, Mama. But I don't think you do, not really. I mean, look at these hands."

Thomas craned his neck to look at them, too. *What was the matter with Mama's hands?* He hadn't noticed anything.

"They used to be the softest, whitest hands in the Tidewater because you never had to do anything but serve tea and curl your hair. But now they're red and chapped and tired—and from what?" He held up the mended shirt. "Rolling bandages and making uniforms and who knows what all else." He leaned close to his mother's face. "You know independence can't be won by talk, and you are doing all you can to help the Patriot cause, and so is Papa. Wouldn't you be proud if I were doing the same thing?"

Thomas couldn't believe what he was hearing. Was Sam actually trying to convince Mama to disagree with Papa and side with *him?* He might as well try to talk her into becoming a Loyalist!

Mama's eyes glistened with tears, and she kissed Sam softly on the forehead. "I'm already proud of you," she said. "I just want peace, in my home as well as in this country."

Sam looked into her round, sad face for a moment and then stood up. "I have to be getting back now," he said stiffly.

Mama watched out the window with the tears still shining until he was out of sight.

Thomas tried not to think about all that as he passed the days, which wasn't hard considering how many other things he had on his mind.

It was a full-time job trying to always be out of the shop when Nicholas Quincy came in or sent for help. People were talking about the doctor like he was some kind of miracle worker.

Still, Thomas didn't want to assist him. *What if I don't know the medicine he wants?* Thomas would ask himself when he was hiding in Francis's cellar. *What if I can't understand what he's talking about with his newfangled treatments? I don't want to go out there and look stupid and clumsy in front of everyone in Williamsburg!*

It was hard, too, not being able to concentrate when he was studying with Alexander. Alexander himself was trying to be as much fun as always. One day he brought in a model for showing Thomas how the planets moved. Another day he stood on a chair and dropped apples on Thomas while he talked about a man named Isaac Newton.

It would have been like a summer adventure if Thomas hadn't spent almost every minute of it watching Alexander and wondering, *He couldn't be the one stealing the horses, could he?*

"What are you thinking, Thomas Hutchinson?" Alexander demanded one day when they were outside under one of the Hutchinsons' mulberry trees, reading Homer's *Odyssey* aloud to each other. It was Alexander's turn to read, and Thomas's mind had drifted as he'd searched his teacher's face for traces of exhaustion from sneaking around at night, taking people's horses.

"Thomas!" he said again. "You haven't heard a word I've read. Have I lost my charm?"

Thomas shifted guiltily against the mulberry's bark. "No," he said. "I was just . . . thinking."

A deep dimple appeared in each of Alexander's cheeks. "So!" he said. "That's why I didn't recognize the expression on your face!" Then he nudged Thomas with his elbow and added, "Another example of sarcasm, Master Hutchinson."

He went back to reading about Odysseus, but Thomas noticed him looking up from the page more often. Thomas tried to reassure himself that Alexander couldn't possibly know what he was thinking.

But the worst part of the way the summer was unfolding for Thomas was Malcolm's being there. The Scottish boy's presence was like a stone in Thomas's shoe from morning until night.

Malcolm had the stable shining, the water from the well sloshing over the barrel, and the wood chopped and stacked in a fancy pyramid every day when Thomas appeared for morning chores, even if he crawled out before dawn. Esther would look pointedly at Thomas and say Malcolm was the best thing that had ever happened to the family.

The new servant spent most of his days rebuilding a fence for the garden. He'd sit with his sleeves rolled up so anyone passing by could see his muscles working, and he flipped his knife around in all kinds of fancy formations as he shaved the bark off the branches for the railings.

Each day by supper time, when Thomas came home from the apothecary shop and was washing up in the water barrel, Malcolm would stroll across the yard with an old harness that he'd shined up to look like new or a three-legged broiler he'd just made for Esther with a long handle to make it easier for her to cook meats over the fire. He'd smile and swagger, and Thomas would wait for the excited squeals from the kitchen.

As far as Thomas was concerned, Malcolm was a know-it-all and a show-off, yet Malcolm had everyone else eating out of his hand—Burgess, the chickens, even Esther. But the worst one was Caroline.

Every time Thomas found time to meet her for a game of ring toss or an evening's adventure at the Chinese Bridge, she would ask if they couldn't go to Thomas's house instead. And there was no way to play in the garden or the yard without Malcolm wriggling his way into their games. That's where the trouble started for Thomas.

The worst day was one late Saturday afternoon when Francis excused Thomas from the apothecary shop long before dark and he raced to find Caroline. *Malcolm will still be doing his chores this early*, Thomas thought as he dashed down Nicholson Street. *Maybe Caroline and I can have some fun by ourselves for once.*

Of course Caroline wanted to go to the Hutchinsons', but all was quiet when they got to the yard, and Malcolm didn't seem to be anywhere around.

"I'll get us something to eat," Thomas said and slipped into the kitchen. Esther was probably sewing with Mama in a cool part of the house, so he was able to pop two apricots inside his shirt. They weren't quite ripe yet, and Thomas stopped to consider taking a couple of Esther's ginger cakes instead. But on closer examination, they were harder than the apricots.

If Malcolm is so perfect, Thomas thought as he exited the kitchen, *why doesn't he teach Esther how to cook?*

He smiled to himself. Caroline would think that was funny. They'd laugh about it while they ate their snack, and then they would climb one of the trees and spin out a story to play later at the Chinese Bridge. This might turn out to be all right after all.

But the minute he reached the garden, his smile faded. There under one of the blazing crepe myrtles sat Caroline with Malcolm. Her eyes were shining at a piece of pottery Malcolm was displaying for her like a turkey fanning out his feathers for her to admire.

Thomas squeezed the apricots to keep from hurling them at him.

Caroline glanced up as he trudged toward them. "Look, Tom!" she said. "Malcolm has a puzzle jug! Have you ever seen one?"

"Of course," Thomas snapped. Then he added to himself, *At least now I have.*

"So you know how it works, then," Malcolm said. His black eyes drew closer together than ever as he held the jug out to him.

Thomas shook his head. "You're the genius," he said. "You show us."

Malcolm looked at him—and through him—before he held the jug closer to Caroline. "You see all these openin's here, lassie?" He pointed to the front where there were four holes arranged like a clover leaf.

Caroline nodded eagerly.

"And of course you see the two spouts on either side," he went on.

"You'd have to be blind not to," said Thomas. He was squirming with irritation.

Caroline glared at Thomas. "So how does it work, Malcolm?" she asked.

"The trick is to drink from it without spillin' out of any of these openin's."

Caroline's eyes shone up at him, as if he just said he can get to the moon and back, Thomas thought.

"Do you know the trick?" she said to Malcolm.

Before he could stop himself, Thomas blurted out, "Well, who doesn't?"

Malcolm's crow-black eyes locked on his, and Thomas wished he could suck those words back in like they'd never been said. Malcolm knew Thomas didn't have a clue how to even begin.

Malcolm's mouth formed a rectangle, and he held out the jug. "Show us, Master Hutchinson," he said.

It was probably the longest moment in the life of "Master Hutchinson" so far. Everything seemed to slow to a crawl as he took the jug filled with water, plastered his fingers over the holes, and tilted it back with his mouth wrapped around one of the spouts. Water sloshed out over his hand and up his sleeve.

Caroline erupted into laughter.

"What's wrong with this thing!" Thomas cried.

"Nothin' at all!" Malcolm said, happy beads of saliva gathering at the corners of his squared-off smile. "Try again, eh, lad?"

Thomas put his lips against the other spout this time, and at once he felt water crawling up his arm—and rage crawling up his backbone. With an angry fling, he hurled the rest of the water in the jug right into Malcolm's face.

Caroline's laughter froze in the air.

"Tom!" she said. She planted her hands onto her hips. "That was a horrible thing to do!"

"He's a cheater! He's fixed it so it won't work and I'd look like a fool! He always does that!"

"He didn't make you look like a fool. You did that all by yourself!"

"Lassie! Laddie!"

They both looked at Malcolm, who had already used his sleeve to smear off his face and was watching them with amusement dancing in his eyes.

"Suppose I settle the whole matter," he said. He took the jug from Thomas's hand, put his lips between the two spouts, and drank without adding a drop to his drenched shirt. "There's a hidden hole under the handle," he said, as if he were talking to two five-year-olds. "You must cover it up and not use either of the spouts." He looked smugly at Thomas. "Anyone who has ever learned the trick wouldn't be forgettin' that now."

"No!" was all Thomas could think of to shout.

"Yes," Malcolm said calmly.

Caroline flipped her sandy hair back over one shoulder and leveled her eyes at Thomas. "I thought you had stopped being a bully," she said. "But you're doing it again." She sniffed and tossed her hair back over the other shoulder. "I don't keep company with bullies." With her chin in the air, she left the garden.

Before the gate could swing shut behind her, Thomas lunged at Malcolm with his fists flying.

"You *do* make a fool of me!" he shouted. "I hate you!"

But before he could land the first punch, his arms were suddenly pinned behind his back, and he fell to the ground like a load of firewood. Malcolm's wiry body came down on top of him, and a hand like a hammer head nailed his face to the ground and held it there.

Thomas struggled to get up, but nothing would move. He felt something tear at his scalp, and his head was wrenched back. Before it registered that Malcolm had two handfuls of his hair, his face was smashed into the ground again.

"Tell me when you've had your fill, *Master* Hutchinson," Malcolm said, his breath hot next to Thomas's ear. "And I'll let you go."

Thomas clenched the inside of his mouth with his teeth to keep from answering. But when Malcolm pulled his head back by the hair again, he let it go and cried, "Enough!"

Malcolm pushed his head gently down on the dirt and got up. "You're smarter than I thought," he said.

Thomas listened as Malcolm's soles crunched across the gravel to the stable.

And then he lay there and tried not to cry.

✠ ⬥ ✠

Chapter Ten

homas didn't know how long he stayed there, feeling the sweat ooze down his nose and the pain pound in his head. He wasn't sure he would ever be able to get up . . . until he heard Esther holler from the direction of the house: "Mal-colm! Come and have some citron water for that thirst of yours!"

The first clear thought came to Thomas's mind since Malcolm had slammed his face into the ground: *I can't let Esther find me like this. I have to get out of here.*

Gasping against the throbbing in his head—and arms and knees—Thomas got to his feet somehow and stumbled behind the laundry building. As soon as Malcolm's shoes had crunched to the kitchen, Thomas held his breath and slipped out between the fence rails.

He pulled what was left of his sleeve across his forehead to wipe the sweat off and looked around for someplace to go.

Maybe I can wash off in the canal, he thought.

But when he glanced down at the arm he'd just dragged

across his face, his heart lurched inside him. It wasn't sweat that was dribbling down over his eyebrows. It was blood.

Thomas put his palms up to his face and pulled them away to look at them. Both were covered with sticky red liquid, and even as he stood there, more dropped into his eyes. A wave of nausea rolled right up his throat.

Francis. He was the only one who could take care of this.

It was a thought that came from somewhere else, but Thomas followed it, staggering behind houses and shops to get to the apothecary. He was seeing black spots in front of his eyes by the time he reached for the knob on the side door.

But when he tugged at the handle, the door didn't budge. Of course. Francis had closed the shop early.

Thomas sank down on the step and put his head in his hands. It hurt so much he could hardly see.

Put your head between your knees, Francis always said to patients who had the ghostly white faces of people about to faint. *Put your head between your knees.*

Just before he passed out, he realized it wasn't Francis's voice he heard in his head, but someone else's right beside him. It was that someone else who caught him in his arms before he went limp.

I know that smell, he thought sometime later. *Francis is cleaning the candle globes with ammonia again.*

He took in a big whiff and came up gagging.

"That's hartshorn!" he sputtered.

"Yes, it is, thank goodness," said a soft voice.

Thomas looked through the fog in his eyes to see Nicholas Quincy leaning over him.

"I think it's done its work," the doctor said.

Thomas sank back down on whatever he was lying on and closed his eyes.

"Where am I?" he asked.

"Mister Pickering's examination room," Nicholas said. "Thank the Lord I had a key."

"What would have happened if you hadn't?" Thomas asked, his eyes still closed.

"You would have bled all over Mister Pickering's steps, and you know how he is about the look of things."

Thomas pried open his eyes. Dr. Quincy's face was still as pale as the moon, but there was a twinkle playing across it. It hurt to look at it. It hurt to look at anything. Thomas closed his eyes again.

"What's that?" he said as he felt something damp and soothing go across his forehead.

"Soapwort for the scraping up you've gotten," Dr. Quincy said. "Then I'll put on a plaster of dovesdung to bring down the swelling while we apply some ground tansy seed and oil for the sore muscles you're going to have before long."

"That bad, is it?" Thomas said.

"You will look worse than you feel."

Thomas's eyes sprang open. "No!" he cried. "I can't look worse! No one can know I've been fighting!"

Nicholas pressed his thin lips together, and Thomas groaned inside. *Why did I tell this sissy that?* he scolded himself. *He doesn't understand about fighting. He'll run to Papa the minute he comes home!*

"I've heard tell that bedstraw, added to oil, will encourage healing and keep the scabs from coming." Nicholas cocked his head. "I have never tried it, but if you're willing, it might mean you'll be healed before your father comes home."

Thomas's deep-set eyes met Nicholas's pale ones. Nicholas just watched him and waited.

"We might try it," Thomas said finally. "I just . . . I just don't want my father to be disappointed in me, you see."

"Bedstraw is believed to have been the manger herb in the hay where the Christ child lay," Nicholas said. "I think that speaks highly of it."

Thomas lay back on Francis's examining table and watched in silence as Nicholas put together a mixture and smoothed it over Thomas's forehead, elbows, and knees. He applied the dovesdung plaster on top of it as if he were laying soft tufts of lamb's wool on his skin, and then went to work mixing up tansy seed for later.

It was quieter than Thomas had ever known the apothecary shop to be, but it wasn't an uncomfortable silence. It made Thomas think of mornings on the plantation when he used to wake up early and have time to lie in bed and smell Cook's johnny cakes baking. So many things had changed since then.

"We'll need to leave that poultice on for a little while," Nicholas said into the silence. "But that will surely raise some questions at home, eh?"

Thomas nodded.

"Why don't you ride out to the Digges's plantation with me and assist me?" Nicholas said.

Thomas felt as if his stomach were turning over. What if he didn't know what to do? What if someone died because he was a clumsy oaf? What if Nicholas just sent him back to the wagon in disgrace? And why now, when he had his skinned-up face to worry about?

"We can take the plaster off when we come back, before you go home," Nicholas said. He gave a brittle laugh. "I'm not much good with a comb, but perhaps between the two of us we can find a way to cover the worst of it with your hair, eh?"

Thomas knew he was staring at the doctor with his mouth open, but he couldn't stop himself. *Is this timid doctor going to help me keep a secret from my family?*

"It's not . . . it's not that I'm afraid, you understand," Thomas stammered.

"Of course not," Nicholas said.

Thomas wasn't sure, but he thought he caught a trace of sarcasm in Nicholas's voice. It didn't matter, though. This had to be better than catching it from everyone from Esther on up.

"All right, then," he said.

And so at the edge of sunset, Thomas waited in Nicholas's wagon while the doctor dashed up to the Hutchinsons' door and told Esther that Thomas would be with him for the rest of the evening. Esther stretched her neck out as far as she could to see just what kind of transportation this new doctor had for himself, and Thomas tried to keep his head down. His ear twinged at the very thought of what Esther would do if she found out he'd been fighting—especially with her beloved Malcolm.

Maybe I should tell them what he did to me, Thomas thought bitterly. *Maybe then they wouldn't all think he was such a prince.*

But would they believe him? Thomas shook his head. Better to do it this way, even if it meant sharing a secret with this lily-livered doctor.

The Digges's plantation was to the east of Williamsburg, out Jamestown Road. The wagon, pulled by an ancient gray mare Nicholas called Dolly, rocked and creaked as they rode, and because Nicholas, as usual, had nothing to say, Thomas busied himself with watching the countryside go by. Once a great blue heron flapped heavily over the surface of a bog. The cricket chorus started to sing, and the dense forest air grew cool and smelled of pine.

"When I left Pennsylvania, I thought I was leaving all the beauty behind," Nicholas said. "But I guess God can make any place beautiful in His own way." He paused for a moment, then added, "Here's something else to think about . . ."

Thomas found himself cocking his head back at Nicholas. "Yes, sir?" he mumbled.

"Understand why I am not going to tell your father about your fighting." Nicholas stared straight ahead as he talked. "It's because I hate to see a young man punished for something he never plans to do again anyway."

It took a moment for that to soak into Thomas's mind.

"You see, I don't believe in fighting. I don't think you do anymore either." Nicholas smiled at him shyly.

He won't tell Papa, Thomas thought, *as long as I agree never to fight again. Who does he think he is?!*

But there was no time for thinking thoughts of anything except medicine when they got to Peyton Digges's room on the second floor of his plantation mansion. Peyton was tossing his salt-and-pepper-colored head from side to side on the pillow, and he was drenched with sweat from side whiskers to toenails.

Nicholas straightened up from Peyton's bed and looked at

Thomas. "Let us see what we can do," he said. There was a firmness in his voice Thomas had never heard there before. It didn't allow for any clumsiness.

"Will you need the rattlesnake root?" Thomas said.

Nicholas nodded. "And we'll need some linens soaked in hot water as well."

Thomas didn't know what those were for, but it struck him as he hurried down the stairs that he didn't need to know. Going right to work on Peyton Digges like he had, Nicholas wasn't the cowering hound dog at the door he usually appeared to be. *I'll know what to do—just from watching him,* Thomas knew.

When he returned from the laundry building with a pile of hot, wet sheets, he found Nicholas standing beside Peyton with one hand on his forehead and the other on his heart. His eyes were closed, and his lips moved without making a sound.

Is he dead? Thomas almost cried.

But then he heard Nicholas murmur, "Amen." He turned to Thomas and said, "Are you ready?"

Thomas wasn't sure what it was he was supposed to be ready for, but he took a deep breath and said, "Yes, sir."

And he was right. He was ready. For two hours, Thomas worked at Dr. Quincy's side. He wrapped the hot linens around Peyton and held his head while Nicholas touched rattlesnake root to his lips with the end of his handkerchief and whispered soft prayers.

Finally, the sweat dried from Peyton's lined face, and he blinked his eyes back at them. Nicholas nodded with satisfaction and began to pack his bag.

"Is he going to be all right?" Mistress Digges whispered from the doorway.

"Yes, ma'am," Nicholas said simply. "But if the fever burns again and he begins to perspire like that," Nicholas said quietly, "you must send for me at once. Until I arrive, do what you saw me do here. I'll leave some rattlesnake root for you."

Mistress Digges nodded and dabbed at her eyes.

"He could do with some bee balm tea if you have any," Nicholas added.

Peyton tugged at the doctor's sleeve, and Nicholas leaned over to put his ear next to the man's lips. When he stood up, he said, "Thomas, perhaps you should go down and have some, too, eh?"

Thomas remembered his own injuries for the first time since they'd arrived, and suddenly he did feel a little wobbly in his knees. As he followed Mistress Digges down the elegant staircase, he realized he also had another feeling, a warm one that wrapped around his chest somehow.

On the way back to Williamsburg, Thomas's head lolled sleepily as the wagon rocked, but he was still thinking his own thoughts. He turned to look at Nicholas, and for an instant, he thought he was dreaming.

The profile that was carved out against the midnight-blue sky wasn't the face of a sissy. The chin was strong. The eyes were alert. And the face looked calm, like the man who wore it had just done something very good.

"You *do* believe in fighting," Thomas said.

Nicholas looked at him in surprise before he shook his head.

"Yes, you do," Thomas insisted. "You just fought hard for Peyton Digges's life."

Nicholas's quiet mouth twitched into a smile. "Ah," he

said. "I suppose that kind of fighting is all right. I'm taking my orders from God, then, you see."

"Oh," Thomas said. He thought some more, and then he looked into his palms and said, "I won't do any of the other kind of fighting anymore, sir."

"Nicholas," the doctor said.

"What?"

"Nicholas. Not *sir*. And Thomas?"

"Yes."

"Thank you. And thank God."

✝ ✦ ✝

Chapter Eleven

𝕴t was hard to sleep that night with the plaster gone and the night air making his forehead sting. Thomas had slipped up the stairs without waking Mama, but after looking in the glass in the dining room when he came in, he was sure she wouldn't have noticed his wounds. What with the darkness and the bedstraw oil and the way Nicholas had combed his hair, no one would ever know.

Except Malcolm.

Thomas was lying in bed thinking his own thoughts about the Scottish servant boy—wondering how he would ever face his sneering smile again after he'd beaten him in his own fight—when he heard a thundering noise outside.

Wincing from the pain in his arms and legs, Thomas brushed past the mosquito netting and hurried stiffly to his front window. He pushed the curtain aside just in time to see a horse leave the Palace Green and gallop around the church, careening as if to go down Jamestown Road.

Thomas rubbed his eyes and looked again. The horse—

and its rider—had disappeared, leaving only a cloud of dust that hung heavily in the boggy air.

But Thomas stared after it for a long time. *Who would that have been, riding about after midnight?* he wondered. Yet that wasn't what bothered him most. There was something about the way the rider had sat in the saddle and taken the corner at such a rakish angle. It was as if the horse didn't want to go that way.

A thought struck Thomas that made him lean out the window to peer into the darkness. Had that been someone stealing another horse?

Had it been Alexander?

He turned back to his bed. That was a thought he didn't want to think.

But there was no getting around it the next morning. Thomas slept until it was almost time for lessons and had to scurry to throw on a mended shirt and comb his hair down over his forehead. He could barely walk down the stairs for the stiffness in his knees, but a look in the dining room glass while Alexander was pulling books from his bag assured him that his face wasn't swollen anymore. Now, if Alexander just wouldn't ask him any questions about it.

He needn't have worried. Alexander was unusually quiet as he spread some new ciphering problems out on the table. He didn't look as if he'd gotten much more sleep than Thomas had. Thomas's heart sank.

"Will you read the first one aloud, Master Hutchinson?" Alexander asked—with none of his usual excitement about arithmetic.

Thomas read, "'If a farmer's wife wanted to dye her wool red and needed one quart of pokeberries boiled in one quart of water for every 20 yards of thread, how many pokeberries must she gather to dye 100 yards of thread?'"

Thomas kept his eyes on Alexander as he divided 100 by 20 in his head. "Five quarts," he replied.

Alexander looked at him blankly.

"Five quarts," Thomas said again. "Isn't that right?"

Alexander sighed. There were no deep dimples in either of his cheeks.

"I'm sorry, Thomas," he said. "I'm having trouble concentrating this morning. That devil Xavier Wormeley was pounding on our door hours before dawn, pointing his finger at us again. It seems Peter Pelham's horse was taken in the night." Alexander ran his hands through his hair. "Why would my father and I be fool enough to risk stealing the jailer's horse?"

Thomas's mind reeled. Then it *was* a stolen horse he'd seen galloping under his window during the night! The rider had to be someone with a way with horses—someone young and strong—to get the steed out of the *jailer's* stable. Alexander could do it. . . .

"Thomas?"

Thomas's head jolted up.

"Have you been embroiled in some kind of battle?"

Thomas's hand went to his forehead. His mouth wouldn't work.

"You look as if you're fighting the British themselves with that expression on your face," Alexander went on. "Is there some struggle you have going on inside that you want to talk about?"

Thomas could only shake his head.

He was on his way out the front door to go to Francis's shop that day after dinner, when Mama floated halfway down the steps in a cool, filmy pink sacque and called, "Thomas, darling, may I ask a favor of you before you leave?"

Thomas nodded and kept his face turned away—just in case.

"Would you go out and ask Malcolm to pick the last of the cherries for supper? I think we need something cool in this heat, and I forgot to ask him this morning."

Thomas felt his heart stop, but he nodded again and headed for the back hall.

"And darling?" Mama leaned over the banister. "Please get your hair out of your face. You are so much more handsome with it brushed back."

Thomas bolted out the back door and ran, knees screaming out in pain the whole way.

Malcolm was sitting in the shade outside the kitchen building, cutting white oak into strips to make a basket for Esther. He looked up when he heard Thomas coming and pulled his knife slowly across the piece of leather on his knee.

Here it comes, Thomas thought miserably. *He'll try to impress me with that knife while he teases me about losing the fight. But I promised Nicholas. I can't get into another one.*

Thomas chomped down on the inside of his mouth and kept going until he came to Malcolm's side.

"Mama wants cherries for supper," he said, heading for the gate.

"Wait," Malcolm said behind him.

Thomas stopped and stiffened. For a terrified second, he thought, *Is he going to jump on me again?*

"I have a message for you," Malcolm said.

Thomas didn't turn around. "From who?"

"Caroline. She came early this mornin' to tell you herself, but you didn't come down for chores."

"I was up late," Thomas started to say, and then stopped himself. *I don't have to explain myself to you*, he thought bitterly. But he was still cautious as he turned to face Malcolm. "So what did she say?"

"Something about bein' sorry . . . and wantin' you to help her because another horse was stolen and that fat magistrate is still accusin' her father and brother."

Thomas sighed slowly. She was sorry. He was, too. Maybe they were still going to be friends after all.

"That must have been the horse I heard barrelin' down the Green after midnight," Malcolm said. "I wish now that I had gotten up and followed him. I *knew* it was a thief."

Thomas felt the hairs on the back of his neck prickling up. "How did you know just by hearing it?"

"I've heard horses bein' stolen before," Malcolm said, slitting another piece of oak with his knife. "The horse and rider didn't know each other, and the rider wasn't givin' the horse time to get used to him."

Thomas didn't say anything. He'd thought almost the same thing himself.

"One thing is sure," Malcolm went on. "I'll be keepin' an extra careful eye on Burgess and Musket, and on Judge when your father brings him back. You can all be certain no Hutchinson horse is goin' to be stolen as long as I'm here!"

Malcolm's eyes glowed, and he set his square mouth as if he were planning to hold back the entire British army.

Then he gave his knife a twirl and stabbed it into the oak with a flourish. Thomas rolled his eyes and stomped off.

Only Francis was in the shop when Thomas got there, and he felt a little dip of disappointment when he learned that Nicholas had gone out to the Digges's plantation to check on his patient.

"He said you were a help to him last night," Francis said. He squinted through his spectacles. "I thought you'd make an apothecary, but now it seems you have your sights set on being a doctor."

Thomas felt a warm flush go through him, and he backed toward the hallway to get his broom, knocking over a tray of surgical instruments in the process.

"Then again, you'll have to get better acquainted with your arms and legs before you do either one," Francis added dryly. "It looks like the last fall you took nearly wiped your face right off your head."

Thomas put his hand up to his forehead and gulped.

"Of course," Francis said, "it takes a trained eye to see it. The hair is a good disguise for the average person who knows nothing about injuries."

Thomas looked at him quickly. The old eyes were twinkling behind the spectacles.

"Go on, now!" Francis barked then. "Off to work!"

Thomas had barely finished his sweeping when Francis handed him a package he'd wrapped himself and said, "It's time for a refill on Mistress Betsy Taylor's medicine."

Thomas only narrowly missed toppling over Francis's mortar and pestle getting to the door. As he bolted out of the shop, he could hear Francis Pickering muttering to himself, "He'll break his neck before his face can heal."

But Thomas didn't care. This was a chance to make sure Caroline wasn't mad at him anymore—and to tell her that it was Malcolm who was the bully, not him.

As soon as the Taylors' back door opened, though, he knew that was the last thing on Caroline's mind. Her brown eyes were swimming with tears again.

"Tom!" she cried. "Papa and Alexander are both away, and Mama's worse—much worse!"

She grabbed his hand and hauled him upstairs.

"It'll be all right, Caroline," Thomas said. "I have more of her medicine."

Still, he stopped and smothered a gasp when he saw Caroline's mother, flopping around in her bed like a trout in the canal. Her miles of golden hair were stuck to her head with perspiration, and there was no welcoming smile when she saw him. In fact, he wasn't sure she saw him at all. Her eyes were cloudy, and they bounced around the room as if something were after her.

"Look at her, Tom!" Caroline whispered. She wrung his hand like a rag. "Can you do something?"

"I . . . I'm not sure," Thomas said.

The only thing he could think of to do was to run for Francis, but that was out of the question—not with Xavier Wormeley watching the Taylor house for galloping bands of horse thieves.

Betsy Taylor flailed her hands wildly, and one of them caught on Thomas's arm. Her skin was sizzling like a roast on a spit. Just the way Peyton Digges's had done.

Suddenly, Dr. Quincy's words roared through his head: *If the fever burns again and he begins to perspire like that, you must send for me at once. Until I arrive, do what you saw me do here.*

Caroline was crying hard now and clutching at her mother's hands and saying, "Mama, Mama, talk to me!"

"Caroline!" Thomas said. "She needs Dr. Quincy! You have to run and fetch him."

"Where is he?"

Thomas felt the bottom drop out of his stomach. "Digges's plantation."

"What?!"

His mind spinning, Thomas dragged Caroline to the door and whispered as fast as he could. "I'll have to go and fetch him. Heat some water in a kettle and get some linens hot. Wrap her in them and get drops of rattlesnake root juice into her mouth. And—"

Thomas stopped and chewed on his lip. What else had Nicholas done? There was something else. . . .

"And what, Tom?"

He remembered.

"Pray," he said. "Pray the whole time."

From the bed, Betsy groaned and cried out, "Robert, hide! They've come for you—please hide!"

Caroline ran to her and flung her arms around her until she grew quiet again.

"I'm going for the doctor," Thomas said.

"Wait, Tom. You know Malcolm can ride faster. Why don't you send him on Burgess?"

"I can do it—"

"This is no time to be a stubborn, foolish, jealous boy!" Caroline's words came out in sobs. "Send Malcolm, *please*. I don't want Mama to die!"

Thomas bit the inside of his mouth and ran.

It didn't take long to convince Malcolm to go after Nicholas Quincy and even less time for the Scottish boy to saddle up Burgess and mount. But when he took up the reins, with Mama, Esther, and Otis all standing around telling him to hurry, he looked down at Thomas with a puzzled frown.

"Where is it that I'm to be goin'?" he asked.

"Digges's plantation. You know, out Jamestown Road."

Malcolm shook his shaggy head. "No, I don't know. I've not been out of Williamsburg since I arrived."

Mama, Esther, and Thomas all started babbling directions at the same time, until Otis put up a gnarled hand and everyone looked. "You go with him," he said to Thomas. "Point the way."

Before anyone could argue, Otis was steering Thomas toward the bay, and he had no choice but to climb on behind Malcolm.

"Hold on, Thomas!" Mama cried frantically.

Thomas clutched at the back of Malcolm's homespun shirt, and they set off at a gallop.

"That way, to the left of the college!" Thomas shouted.

Malcolm nodded and bent low over Burgess's neck. Thomas bent with him. There was no room in his head for thinking about anything but getting the doctor for Betsy.

I hope Caroline has those sheets warmed and is giving her the rattlesnake root—and praying, Thomas thought. *I should be there helping her. I'm worthless here!*

He wasn't sure where the thought came from, but it suddenly came into his mind that at least he could pray, too. He wasn't sure he remembered how. His mind had been so cluttered up with confusion and suspicion and changing rules, he hadn't been able to talk to God. But as he clung to Malcolm and rode up Jamestown Road faster than he'd ever ridden on a horse before, the words just came to him.

Please, God, I know I haven't been talking to You, but this isn't for me, it's for Betsy Taylor, and for Caroline. Please, please, please don't let Betsy die. Please let us get to Nicholas on time. Please.

He stopped praying only long enough to shout, "This way! A little ways down this road!"

Malcolm just nodded and spurred Burgess on even faster. Thomas could see the sweat glowing on the horse's sides.

Thomas was on the ground before Malcolm even brought Burgess to a stop. He ran for the door. Mistress Digges had it open the minute he began to pound.

"We saw you flying up the road, honey!" she cried. "What's wrong?"

Thomas was trying to sputter out an explanation when Nicholas flew down the stairs with his bag in his hand.

"Who is it?" he said.

"Betsy Taylor on Nicholson Street," Thomas gasped out. "Fever."

Without a word or a nod, Nicholas raced out the door, and they heard his horse's hooves beating on the dusty road toward Williamsburg.

"God be with you!" Mistress Digges called out behind him as Thomas tore for Burgess and flung himself back on.

"Let's go!" he shouted to Malcolm. "Can we get back to town as fast as we got here?"

"Hardly," Malcolm said over his shoulder. "This horse will drop dead if we run him any more in this heat. We need to be gettin' him to water as soon as we can."

"But I have to get back to Betsy!"

Malcolm picked up the reins and clucked softly to Burgess. "The way that doctor was ridin', he'll be there before we get out to the end of the plantation road. In the meantime, she has Caroline and your mother."

And God, I hope, Thomas thought. He sighed impatiently. *At least at this pace I don't have to hold on to Malcolm.*

Malcolm reined Burgess off Jamestown Road where the river stood as still as a painting in the afternoon heat. Burgess ducked his head into the water and lapped it up. Malcolm slumped lazily against a poplar tree and picked up a piece of grass to chew on.

Thomas planned to stand and pace until they were ready to go, but the humid air was like a hand in a woolen glove pressing on him. He had to sink down in the shade near Malcolm because there was no other refuge from the sun. But he sat with his back to him.

There was a long, uncomfortable silence. And then, cutting through it as if his voice were one of his fancy knives, Malcolm said, "So, Master Hutchinson, why do you hate me so much?"

☦ ⁌ ☦

Chapter Twelve

In spite of the steaming heat, Thomas froze to the spot. No one had ever asked him a question like that before . . . and certainly no one who had the ability to grind his face into the ground.

"Well?" Malcolm said.

Thomas glanced over his shoulder. "If I tell you, are you going to jump on me again?"

"Only if you jump on me first. That's the way it's always worked before, eh?"

Thomas turned all the way around to look at him. Malcolm's voice didn't sound sarcastic or even angry. The black eyes that looked back at him were open wide, as if he were really expecting an answer.

"Tell me why you're hatin' me so," Malcolm said again.

"I don't want to talk about it," Thomas said.

"Coward."

"I'm not!"

"Then have the courage to tell me why. Do you always

hate those lower than you?"

"No one is lower than anyone else," Thomas said automatically. "That's what the war for independence is all about."

Malcolm snickered softly. "That would explain why I sleep in the servants' quarters behind your house on a pallet of straw while you're in a soft bed inside."

Now he's being sarcastic, Thomas thought. He said to Malcolm, "That isn't why I hate you."

"Then why do you?"

"Because you're a know-it-all and a show-off!" The words blasted out of Thomas with such force that he thought for a minute Malcolm's face would blister up and peel off.

And then Malcolm stuck the grass between his teeth again and said, "That's funny, lad. I thought the same thing about you."

They stared long and hard at each other, and Thomas was never certain what would have happened next if a horse hadn't charged out of a thicket of trees on the other side of the road. The animal was drawn up for a moment, and its black flanks heaved in and out with exhaustion and heat.

Thomas gasped out loud and then clapped his hand over his mouth. The rider sitting tall in the saddle was wearing a black cloak and hood—and a mask that covered his entire face.

In a moment of decision, the rider kicked out his heels and slammed them into the horse's sides, and they were gone again, on down Jamestown Road like a spark shooting out of a fire.

"The horse thief," Thomas said, more to himself than to Malcolm.

"I'm sure of it," Malcolm said—so fiercely that Thomas peered at him closely. He stood up, fists wrenched at his sides.

Thomas watched, ready to spring up—and run—if it looked as if Malcolm were going to turn those fists on him.

"Why else would the blighter be wearin' a cloak and hood in this weather?" Malcolm said. "If Burgess weren't so wore out I'd be after him, I would. I'd love to see the miserable creature caught, and I'd love to be the one to do it! We can't let anythin' stand in the way of the Patriots' cause!"

Thomas stared at him. "We?"

Malcolm jutted out his sharp chin. "I consider myself a Patriot."

"But you just got here!"

"That doesn't mean I've been livin' in a cave the last five years. Every time we got word of the war, I was there, takin' it all in. And I read all I can about it, every chance I get."

Thomas blinked. "But why?"

Malcolm dropped to the ground again and selected another piece of grass. "You said it yourself. This war is all about nobody bein' better nor lower than anybody else. I have always been lower. I'd like to be equal."

Thomas poked at a tuft of weeds with his toe. "Then why are you always trying to prove that you're better than me?"

"Not better," Malcolm answered. "But just as good." He looked sideways at Thomas. "You're the first boy who ever came close to bein' as good a fighter as I am. I hope I didn't hurt you too bad, lad."

Thomas shrugged, but he couldn't help putting his hand to his forehead and brushing his hair back. Malcolm let out a long, slow whistle.

"I only did that because I was afraid you would do worse to me if I let you," Malcolm said. "That's the way I had to fight where I come from." His black eyes had lost their sharpness, and even his mouth didn't look quite as square.

"I'll be fine," Thomas said. "As long as my father doesn't find out. He hates fighting."

"So do I. But sometimes the anger—it just burns up from my toes."

Thomas felt his eyes bulge. "And it makes the back of your neck stiff?"

Malcolm nodded. "Then all of a sudden you're punchin' some poor fellow until he can't stand up."

"Or until someone pulls you off him."

Malcolm shook his head—rather sadly, Thomas thought. "That's never happened to me," he said. "No one cared enough to do that."

Everything was quiet for a minute, except for Burgess gently chomping on the clover and the frogs warming up for their evening concert. Then Malcolm rolled over onto his stomach and said, "You're thinkin' that was your teacher on that horse, aren't you?"

Thomas stiffened all over again. "Alexander? In the mask? No!"

But Malcolm just nodded. "I don't blame you for bein' mad. I know how it is to be suspicious of people you thought you could trust . . . and even to find out for sure that they're thieves."

Thomas tried to protest again, but his mind flipped back to everything that had happened today. . . .

Alexander looking as if he hadn't slept all night.

Alexander and his father being away from home—again— just when this last horse was probably stolen.

Betsy Taylor crying out, "Robert, hide! They've come for you!"

The masked rider sitting tall in the saddle, just the way strong, young Alexander would.

Thomas scrambled up from the ground and dusted off the back of his breeches. "Is Burgess ready to go back now?"

Malcolm nodded without a word.

When they rode into the Taylors' yard, the candles were already flickering in the windows. Betsy Taylor's room was alive with the light of happy faces, and the brightest came from Betsy herself. Although she was still pasty white, she beamed at Thomas.

"You saved the day again, Thomas Hutchinson," she said in a tiny voice. "Where have you been hiding this wonderful doctor?"

Nicholas, of course, busied himself with his bag as if he wished he were anyplace else.

"He is wonderful!" Virginia Hutchinson sang out with her usual charm. "But I think we must also thank God for Caroline here and for our two messengers."

"Who is this handsome young man, Virginia?" Betsy asked.

They all looked at Malcolm.

Handsome? Thomas thought, gazing at Malcolm's badly cut hair and too-close-together eyes while the introductions were made. *Betsy Taylor must still be delirious!*

He glanced at Caroline, who was busy looking from Thomas to Malcolm and back again with a big wedge of a smile on her face. There seemed to be a thousand dimples in each of her cheeks.

A voice filled the room from the doorway and Alexander burst in, followed by his father. "A party? And no one invited me?"

Serious Robert Taylor rushed to his wife's bedside, while Alexander tried to sort out the jumble of explanations he was getting from Mama, Caroline, and Betsy herself. Nicholas slipped silently out. Thomas stared at Alexander and his father.

Both of them were red-faced. Both of them were breathing like a pair of blacksmith's bellows. Both of them smelled of leather and horsehair.

Thomas tried not to look at Malcolm. When he did, he could tell that Malcolm had seen it, too.

Please, God, Thomas prayed as he looked away. *Don't let them be the ones. Please.*

Suddenly, there was a pounding below them, as if someone were trying to beat down the front door from the outside. Alexander went to the front window and leaned out, with Thomas and Malcolm crowding in behind him. Floppy-jowled Xavier Wormeley squinted up at them, one fat, sausage-fingered hand shielding his eyes.

"We've had sickness here, Xavier," Alexander called down. "We'll thank you to leave us be."

"You'll have worse than that, Taylor!" Xavier shouted back. His face was black-red—like some of those rotting cherries in the orchard, Thomas thought.

"What is it?" Alexander said impatiently. "Please! My mother is ill."

"I just want you to know that we have not missed your latest theft," the magistrate said. "Isaiah Chowning's horse was stolen just this afternoon, while he was at the tavern tending to his business there. A man cannot even go about his work without worrying about having his goods taken from him!"

"I'm sorry for Isaiah," Alexander said. "Now, good day, sir."

"I'll find proof!" Xavier shouted. Thomas thought surely his jowls would lift him right off the ground, they were flapping so hard. "Mark my words. I'll have you both hanged!"

Alexander slammed the window shut and turned back to the room full of people with a smile that, to Thomas, wasn't very real. Everyone tried to chat merrily again and turn their attention back to Betsy.

But the word "hanged" swung in the air above them like a noose.

It was the next day after work at the apothecary shop before Thomas had a chance to talk to Caroline again. She was waiting for him outside when Francis closed up the shop and let him go.

"Tom, I'm so happy!" she said, her brown eyes dancing.

"Why?"

"Mama's better, for one thing. Dr. Quincy came to visit her again today, and he says she'll be up and tending her roses again in no time. I like him, Tom, don't you?"

Thomas had to nod. He had just spent the afternoon at the doctor's side, learning about some new herbs Nicholas wanted to try using. Even old Francis was less cranky when Nicholas was around.

"And of course I'm happy that you've stopped acting like a ninny and decided to be Malcolm's friend now."

Thomas stopped dead on the road, setting up a cloud of dust around them. "Friend? Where did you get that idea?"

"From Malcolm," she said matter-of-factly. "But I could tell myself the minute you two walked in the door of Mama's room last night. You didn't look as if you wanted to strangle one another!"

"*Malcolm* told you we were 'friends'?"

"Well, not exactly. He said you understand each other now. That's almost the same thing, isn't it?"

Thomas started walking again, arms folded across his chest.

"Well, isn't it?" she repeated.

"Maybe," Thomas said.

Caroline broke into a skip. "Good, because I told him we would be by this evening to see him—the two of us."

Thomas waited for the hair on the back of his neck to stand up, or his fists to clench themselves. But it didn't happen.

I'm not excited about it, mind you, he told himself firmly. *Not at all. I'm only doing this for Caroline.*

Whoever he was doing it for, Thomas had to admit a week later that the summer had taken a turn out of the doldrums and into the sunshine.

Poor Xavier Wormeley. The horse that was "taken" from Isaiah Chowning mysteriously reappeared in his stable sometime during that same night. Alexander said he suspected Isaiah was just trying to make Xavier look like a fool . . . which wasn't too difficult as far as Thomas could see.

And Xavier still had no proof that any of the other horses

had been stolen by the Taylors, and he seemed to be spending most of his time brooding over it inside the courthouse.

Except for Peyton Digges, who still required daily visits, Nicholas had brought everyone who had the fever back to health. Suddenly, he was being invited to Williamsburg houses for festive evening suppers. Mama said she would have him in as soon as Papa came home.

In the meantime, Caroline came by the apothecary shop almost every day with apricot tarts or biscuits spread with plum preserves to share with Thomas, Nicholas, and Francis while the four of them chatted. In his quiet way, Nicholas seemed to love nothing better than to explain the bones on the skeleton in the corner of Francis's examining room or the seed mixture he was testing for rheumatism or gout. Francis put in his two-pence on occasion, until a customer came in and he hustled them all back to work.

No more horses were stolen, which was almost the best part for Thomas. Sometimes when he was doing his lessons with Alexander—reading a passage from Homer without a single mistake or solving a ciphering problem Alexander had assured him with a dimpled smile that he could not do— Thomas would forget that he had ever suspected Alexander of being a thief.

It must have been some Loyalist from Fredericksburg or Richmond who has done his work and gone on his way, Thomas assured himself. That was the theory Alexander had offered, and Thomas was pretty sure it was right.

Pretty sure.

But the absolutely best part of the way the summer was turning out was the Fearsome Trio: Caroline the Courageous,

Thomas the Tireless, and Malcolm the Mighty. They gave themselves those names the first evening Caroline and Thomas took Malcolm to the Chinese Bridge.

Thomas hadn't been in favor of the idea at first, even though the three of them had spent every evening together since the day Betsy Taylor had the fever. After all, the Palace Gardens and the bridge were *their* secret places—his and Caroline's. He hung behind Malcolm and Caroline as they made their way to the bridge that first night, sulking and pouting until he was certain his lip would begin dragging the ground—until they reached the canal.

There, Malcolm asked, "So, what do you do here?"

"We make up games," Caroline said. "You know, imaginary scenes that we play out, like actors on a stage."

Malcolm looked completely bewildered. "I don't know what you mean, lassie."

"You've never pretended to be a warrior or a general or anything?" Caroline asked, her brown eyes as round as they had ever been.

"No," Malcolm said. "Why would I?"

At last, Thomas thought, *something the Amazing Malcolm doesn't know how to do.*

Thomas squared his shoulders and puffed out his chest. "Then we'll show you."

And they did. Before the night was over, they had 15-year-old Malcolm hiding under the bridge playing the troll, crawling through the high grass portraying a wounded soldier, and leaping out of a willow tree acting as "one of those fighters Sam talked about." Thomas didn't know what they were called, but it didn't matter. Malcolm turned out to be a convincing pretender. And on the way home, Thomas had to admit to himself that it was more fun with three. It was even Malcolm who suggested that they needed a name for themselves.

But it was Thomas who came up with the Fearsome Trio. He'd read more books than Malcolm.

And so it was as if someone from one of their imaginary scenes had waved a wand and lifted the spell that had been cast over Williamsburg. As he lay in bed one night, listening to the crickets and the peepers, Thomas began to talk to God, the way he'd remembered to do every night since the day of Betsy Taylor's illness. He stopped in midword and smiled into the darkness.

It wasn't some magical being who had blessed the town. It was God—because he and Mama and Papa and Reverend Pendleton and so many other people were praying.

Thomas squirmed into the bed linen and sighed. Maybe the rules hadn't changed after all. And maybe everything was going to be perfect now.

But he couldn't have been further from the truth.

✢ ✤ ✢

Chapter Thirteen

The next Sunday when Thomas came downstairs for breakfast in the parlor, he found Mama in a white morning dress, fussing with a bowl of apricots, cherries, and plums on the drop-leaf table. Thomas noticed right away—and with a certain amount of delight—that there were no rock-hard biscuits or bowls of gray mush in sight.

"I've prepared our breakfast this morning, darling!" Mama sang out as she stepped back to admire her fruit arrangement.

"Where's Esther?" Thomas asked.

"In bed with a summer cold, poor thing. Malcolm is looking after her, and I'm looking after you!" She looked so proud of herself that even her black curls trembled with the excitement of it all.

You would think she had cooked us a seven-course meal, Thomas thought. But he bit into an apricot and said, "Delicious, Mama."

Her porcelain face shimmered with a smile, but then just as suddenly, she knitted her tiny black eyebrows together and frowned. "But what shall we do about dinner?"

Before Thomas could suggest that they visit the Bake Shop and live off of shrewsbury cakes until Esther recovered, Mama was shimmering again.

"I know!" she announced. "Why don't you children pack a picnic and go down to the river after church?" She was already planning it on her dainty fingers. "You must invite Caroline, of course, and you can take whatever fruit we don't eat now, and I saw some bread in the cupboard still, and surely there is some butter. . . ."

There was really no need to convince Thomas. He spewed out the news to Malcolm as soon as they started the family walk to Bruton Parish Church, and it was all he could do not to call across the aisle to Caroline while they were waiting for the processional to begin.

But it was always quiet in the church before the service started as the people of the parish came up the center aisle and seated themselves in their proper places—the wealthy landowners in the front near the pulpit, the servants and slaves in the left balcony, professors in the right one, and the college students in the rear gallery. Papa always said it was God's blessing that at least in church the slaves, shopkeepers, and landowners were all together in one place, as they were at no other time.

Thomas always spent this time looking around the white, airy church with its curved windows, wondering where Jesus would sit if He came back to attend a service. He often wondered if Jesus would find the seats as uncomfortable as he did. The pews had red cushions to match the ones they knelt on for prayers, but the backs of the pews went straight up, so a person had to sit as stiff as a ramrod during the long sermons Reverend Pendleton delivered from his raised pulpit. Caroline always complained that she could barely see over the low wall that surrounded each pew, but Thomas was too tall to ever have that problem. His was keeping his feet from scraping noisily against the stone floor when he swung them. When Clayton was there, Thomas could always count on him to shoot a black look his way when that happened.

Today, Thomas's eyes wandered to the altar at the front of the church where the reverend stood on the Sundays when they celebrated the Holy Communion. While the pulpit where the sermons were preached looked fit for a king, the altar was simple with only a snowy-white cloth on it.

But it was what hung on the wall behind it that caught Thomas's eye that Sunday. He'd never really focused on them before, but there were three big tablets there, each with words on it, which Thomas couldn't read from where he sat. He would have to ask Alexander about them at lessons tomorrow.

Xavier Wormeley was the last to sail up the aisle to his seat in the front row, as usual. Papa said he only came to church to be seen, rather than to hear God's Word. Thomas straightened in his seat.

I surely don't want to be like Xavier Wormeley, he thought. *It might be worth trying to listen today.*

He told himself later that he really did try. But Edmond Pendleton used such big words and long, complicated sentences that it was hard not to think about the picnic instead. At least he caught a few snatches.

"We must hold the established church together during this time of trial," the reverend said.

"We must continue to be the bulwark of decency.

"And I say we must tolerate those Christians who do not worship with us—the Baptists and the Quakers and such like."

That caught Thomas's ear because Sam had told him the Quakers wouldn't fight in the war.

"It is our duty in this church to make Williamsburg a haven for all decent Christians. If our young men are to fight for liberty, then let us uphold that liberty by allowing free exercise of religion for all."

Xavier Wormeley chose that moment to let out a loud snore from the front pew. Thomas had to bury his face in Mama's sleeve to keep from laughing out loud. That ended his attempt to listen to the Word that day.

After the service, Thomas plowed through the parishioners who stood talking in the aisles to get out to meet Malcolm, and then he stood, first on one foot, then the other, waiting for Caroline to emerge. He knew Betsy Taylor kept a close eye on her to be sure she was practicing ladylike manners, especially in the church.

As they stood there—Malcolm looking starched and uncomfortable in his white shirt and brown Sunday breeches and waistcoat—several people greeted Thomas and asked about his father.

"Do you know everyone in town, then, lad?" Malcolm asked.

"Almost. My father does."

"So where is the doctor?"

Thomas looked around and shrugged. "Now that I think of it, I've never seen Nicholas in church."

"Is he a heathen, then?"

"No!" Thomas said. "He prays for all his patients. I've seen him!"

"All right, then, don't let your kettle boil over," Malcolm said, eyes sparkling.

But Thomas made another survey of the churchyard, hoping to locate Nicholas and prove his innocence to Malcolm. As his eyes scanned the little knots of chattering people, he didn't spot the doctor, but he did see his brother.

"There's Sam!"

"Will you go over and talk to him, then?" Malcolm said.

Thomas shook his head. Sam was with Ulysses Digges and some of his other friends from the college. Whenever Thomas joined their group, Sam usually patted him on the head and went on his way with his companions, who never even acknowledged that Thomas was there. It wasn't Thomas's favorite feeling to watch them walk away, all laughing together and punching and poking at each other in fun.

But Thomas did watch them today long enough to see that they weren't having fun. In fact, Sam seemed to be leading them in a serious conversation.

"What do you guess is goin' on there?" Malcolm wondered aloud.

"I suppose they have important things to talk about," Thomas said. He looked at them longingly, until Malcolm nudged his arm.

"Here comes Caroline," he said.

Then, of course, Sam, Nicholas, and all other serious topics were forgotten as they told Caroline about the picnic and she squealed and begged her mother to let her go. Within the hour, they were dressed in play clothes, armed with a basket overflowing with bread, fruit, and cakes, and perched in the wagon Otis used for hauling grain back from the mill with Malcolm in the driver's seat.

"Have a lovely day!" Mama chirped, leaning out over the gate and waving her handkerchief as if she were sending them off on a six-month journey. "You children work hard in this dark time, and you deserve a day of laughter."

It didn't seem like a dark time to Thomas at all now. The three of them sang all the way to the James River, bumping and bouncing on the wagon seat and laughing between every verse. When they arrived at the river's edge, they piled out of the wagon and ran through the woods shrieking, as if they *had* been on a six-months' journey.

When Thomas announced that he was starving—and Malcolm asked if they should be surprised by that news— Caroline spread a quilt on the ground and played hostess with the picnic basket.

"You'll make someone a fine wife someday, lassie," Malcolm said as he slathered butter on a piece of batter bread.

Thomas curled his lip. "Wife? Ew!"

"You don't think I'll make a good wife, Tom Hutchinson?" Caroline said indignantly.

Malcolm chuckled. "Now you've made a mess of things, lad!"

"I didn't mean that," Thomas said. "I suppose you'll be all right as someone's wife. . . ."

"I would stop now if I were you," Malcolm said. "You're only makin' it worse."

"But if she's a wife, then she'll be no fun anymore. We won't be able to . . . well, go on picnics and hide at the bridge!"

Caroline studied a shrewsbury cake with a puckered brow. "I think that's true, Tom," she said in her of-course way. "My mother certainly doesn't disappear every evening to go running about with her friends! Does yours, Malcolm?"

Malcolm's grin stiffened. "My mother died when I was young. But no, I don't think she did."

There was a silence full of thoughts. *I can't imagine not having a mother*, Thomas told himself. *As silly as she is sometimes, she is my mother!*

"I don't know about you two," Malcolm said suddenly, "but I've about had my fill of food for now. What would you say to a hike through the woods, eh?"

"We can pretend we're explorers!" Caroline said.

"I'll be Captain John Smith!" Thomas cried, getting to his feet and tripping over one of them.

"Who would Captain John Smith be?" Malcolm asked.

Thomas regaled them both with the story of the discovery of nearby Jamestown as they all set off away from the wagon with Malcolm in the lead.

"You be John Smith," Caroline said.

"It will be more realistic if someone who has truly never been here heads the party," Thomas explained.

"Besides," said Caroline, "Tom is likely to lead us into every hole and gully."

Thomas had gotten to only the part in the story where Pocahontas supposedly saved John Smith's life when Malcolm gave a loud "*Shhh!*" and put up his hand for them to stop.

"What is it?" Caroline hissed.

Malcolm shook his head sternly and cocked his head to listen. That's when Thomas heard it, too—the sound of a galloping horse's hooves beating the ground.

"It must be someone traveling Jamestown Road," Caroline said. "Why must we be quiet?"

But Malcolm grabbed her arm and motioned with his head for Thomas to follow them behind a large oak tree.

"They've cut off from Jamestown Road onto a path I saw back there," Malcolm whispered to them.

"So?" Caroline whispered back.

But Thomas knew what Malcolm was thinking. Was this the masked rider again? Had he stolen another horse?

Malcolm quivered as he pulled them close to him to watch. Thomas felt a chill of adventure, too . . . until he thought of something.

What if it's Alexander? What if Caroline sees that it really is her brother who has been doing the stealing? I know how I would feel if it were my brother—

"Maybe we shouldn't stay," Thomas whispered uneasily. "What if he sees us and—"

"He won't see us," Malcolm said. "Just stay low."

Thomas crouched down and gave the inside of his mouth a good chewing. It was too late to run now without being seen. He started praying. *Please, God, don't let it be Alexander.*

A second later, a horseman rounded the curve in the path, and Thomas had to bite harder to keep from crying out.

The rider's black cape blew out around him, and he was wearing a mask. Thomas stared hard at the body that sat in the saddle. Was he too big to be Alexander? His teacher had wide shoulders compared to his slim waist, but he wasn't a large young man. How big was this rider?

But it was impossible to tell with the cape billowing out,

and in a flash, he was past them.

And then he stopped.

Thomas dug his fingers into Malcolm's arm and his teeth into his lip. The masked rider had reined in his horse just five long strides up the path from where they were hiding. Malcolm looked at Thomas and Caroline, and his eyes clearly said, "Stay perfectly still."

Thomas turned himself into a statue as he watched the masked rider. The man dismounted and, looking once over each shoulder, tied the horse's reins to the sturdy branch of another oak. Glancing around him again, he set off at a run and disappeared into the woods on the other side of the path.

For a full minute, the members of the Fearsome Trio held their breath. Malcolm finally stole out from behind the tree and peered off in the direction of the masked rider's escape.

"He's long gone," he whispered.

Thomas straightened out his kinked legs. "That was the same man we saw that day—"

"And it wasn't Alexander!" Caroline cut in. "I know how my brother sits on a horse, and that wasn't him!"

Her eyes were sparkling with happy tears, and Thomas wanted to believe her so badly that he did. Malcolm didn't say anything, but put up his hand again.

"Do you hear another horse?"

Caroline's eye grew round, and Thomas nodded like a pecking chicken as he snatched Caroline's hand and dragged her with him behind the tree again.

They had no sooner squatted into their hiding place when a bony gray mare rounded the curve and slowed to a halt where the other horse was tied.

The rider didn't climb from his saddle but looked around cautiously before he leaned over and untied the horse and rode back in the direction he'd come from, leading the stolen horse beside him.

This rider wasn't wearing a mask, and all three of them saw his face as he turned to ride away.

The rider was Nicholas Quincy.

✝ ⬧ ✝

Chapter Fourteen

𝔍t was a downcast trio that made its way slowly back to Williamsburg that afternoon with a picnic basket still half full of food and hearts overflowing with disappointment.

Malcolm studied the matter in silence, his black eyes narrowed on the road.

Caroline stared down at her lap and nibbled at the ends of her hair.

But neither was as solemn as Thomas. He sat slumped in the back of the wagon with his head in his hands, trying to fight back the tears.

My prayers were answered, all right, he thought angrily. *It wasn't Alexander stealing horses. It was Nicholas!*

He didn't know which was worse—and either one was just as bad as if it had been Sam or Clayton. He tried to bring up a sigh, but a pain in his chest blocked its way.

Just outside of town, with the college barely in sight, Malcolm stopped the wagon along the side of the road and pulled Caroline and Thomas in with the look he gave them.

"We have to decide what to do," he said.

Thomas hadn't thought of that. The pain got sharper.

"We have to tell Xavier Wormeley, don't we?" Caroline said.

"No!" Thomas cried.

"But that would make him leave Alexander and Papa alone!"

"Perhaps not, lassie," Malcolm said. "We still don't know who the man in the mask is."

Caroline crossed her arms over the front of her yellow-flowered dress. "It wasn't Alexander," she said.

"But who's going to believe you?" Malcolm asked softly. "You're his sister."

"So what do we do?" Thomas said. So far, all he had been able to think of was telling Papa—and Papa wasn't here.

"I think we should keep it to ourselves for a while," Malcolm said. "Just until we know more."

"But we saw Nicholas!" Caroline said. "It isn't right not to tell!"

"Maybe there's another reason why he took that horse!" Thomas sputtered. "Maybe he was just riding by and saw it and thought it was lost. . . ."

His voice trailed off as both Malcolm and Caroline looked at him. No one had to remind him that the horse was tied to a tree, and that Nicholas had seemed to know exactly where he was going and what he was going to do.

"So what do you mean by 'know more'?" Caroline asked.

"Who the masked horseman is, for one thing," Malcolm said.

She threw up her hands. "Who's going to tell us that?"

"No one," Malcolm said. He twitched a dark, bushy eyebrow. "We can find out for ourselves. After all, we're the Fearsome Trio."

"But that's just for play," Thomas said. "We're only pretending."

"If you pretend it, you can probably do it," Malcolm said.

A chill ran through Thomas. He didn't know whether it was from fear or excitement—and he didn't know what to say. But Caroline did.

"All right, then," she said. "But if Xavier Wormeley comes and takes Alexander and Papa off to jail, we have to tell!"

The boys nodded solemnly. Malcolm put out his hand and they both took it and squeezed it. He put on a square smile.

"All right. Thomas the Tireless, you see Dr. Quincy the most. Find out what you can from him." He saluted sharply to Thomas, and for a moment Thomas had to smile. Malcolm was trying hard to make this easier for them. Clearing his throat, Malcolm said, "Caroline the Courageous, you listen for clues from your brother."

"But he didn't—"

"I know! But just listen anyway."

"What are *you* going to do, Mighty Malcolm?" Thomas asked.

"I don't know yet," he said.

But in spite of Malcolm's playful shrug, Thomas didn't believe him for a minute.

It was impossible to sleep that night with the questions circling his mind. Thomas could only lie inside the mosquito netting, drenching his bed linens with sweat.

It still didn't seem right, not telling some grown person about Nicholas. But then, it didn't seem any more right to think of Nicholas Quincy going off to jail. How could that gentle man, that miracle worker who prayed over his patients—how could he be a thief?

Yet they had watched him take the horse with their own eyes, just as if he had schemed with the masked rider all along. Maybe he had a good reason, but what could that possibly be?

Isn't stealing just wrong? Thomas thought as he punched his pillows up and flopped over for the hundredth time. *Don't some rules stay the same? Where is the rule I'm supposed to follow right now?*

Thomas heard the rooster crow before he finally fell asleep, and he was awakened again long after daylight by a deep voice coming from the parlor below his room. He barely had his eyes pried open before he realized who it was. Papa!

Thomas wriggled out of his nightshift and into his shirt and breeches and lumbered down the stairs with his shoes and stockings in his hand.

Esther clucked at him as he whipped past her. "First you don't get up in time to help Malcolm with the chores, then you come to breakfast half dressed—and me an ailin' woman—"

"Papa's home!" he flung over his shoulder.

"Ah," she said dryly, "that explains everything." And then for good measure, she sneezed.

Thomas dropped his shoes in the parlor doorway and flew across the room. Papa stood up and engulfed him in a hug that Thomas didn't want to let go of. He could feel his father's strength right through his waistcoat. Everything was going to be all right now.

"What's this now?" Papa said, holding Thomas out at arm's length to look at him. "I've only been gone a few weeks. You'd think I'd been away a year!"

"It seems like it, sir!"

Papa held out a chair with one big hand. "Will you join me for breakfast?"

"I don't know if there's time," Thomas said. "I have lessons."

"Alexander left word that he would be late in arriving this morning. Something about a family matter."

What kind of family matter? Thomas wondered. *Did Caroline lose her nerve and tell about Nicholas? Did Xavier Wormeley come and fetch her father off to jail?*

Thomas shook his head. This was the first time he had been alone with his father since last spring, just before Papa had gone off to Newport. He didn't want to spend this precious hour thinking about other things.

While they chiseled through Esther's hoe cake and downed tankards of fresh milk—what damage could a person do to milk, Papa said with a twinkle—Papa asked about his lessons with Alexander, how he was getting on with Malcolm, and what he might have learned from the new doctor.

Thomas could feel his face burning bright red at that last question, and he was certain his father could see the guilt it painted.

"What news do you have, Papa?" Thomas said, fumbling for his tankard.

Papa's face clouded. "Not much that is good. While I was in Richmond trying to buy materials for my shipbuilding project, I sat in on the Virginia Congress for a bit." He shook his head. "There is so much fussing and fighting going on among the members here, I don't know how we will ever fend off the British if they come to Virginia. But—" his eyes lit up "—I have one bit of good news to report. Two, actually. George Mason has written a Bill of Rights for the Virginia Constitution, and he has included religious freedom. Edmond Pendleton will be glad to hear that."

"He preached about free—" Thomas tried to summon up the words "—free exercise of religion, I think, yesterday."

His father nodded his gray-streaked head in approval. "Good. You're listening. If you listen to your teachers, your minister, and your parents—and your God—you can never go wrong, Thomas."

That sounded like too much to listen to for Thomas, at least right now. "What was the other piece of news?"

"Ah. George Mason also included freedom of press in his Bill of Rights."

"What is that?" Thomas said.

"It states that people will be free to write and publish the truth, even if it disagrees with the government."

"Do you like that rule?"

"I like it very much. In order to be free to think for yourself, you need to know more. A free press gives you that."

Thomas thought, *That's what I need. Then I can decide—*

He stopped and felt the burn on his face again. His father was studying him with his piercing blue eyes.

"What is it, son?" he asked. "You brought some trouble into this room as clearly as if you carried it in a satchel. Come on, then. What is in your mind?"

Thomas felt as if he were clawing around in his brain.

What should I do? I promised I wouldn't tell on Nicholas, but this is Papa!

More than that, Thomas didn't want to lie. The only person in the world who could possibly help him out of this sticky web was his father. And maybe he still could . . . without knowing everything.

Thomas took a deep breath. "I just wanted to ask you a question, sir," he said slowly.

His father sipped his milk and waited.

"The rules are changing. You just said even the Virginia Congress is making new ones."

Papa nodded.

"Does that mean that things that used to be wrong aren't wrong anymore?"

"I'm somewhat confused, Thomas," John Hutchinson said. "Perhaps you could explain."

I can't! Thomas wanted to shout. But he went on anyway.

"It used to be wrong to belong to any other church but the Church of England. But now it's all right to be a Baptist or a Quaker. So, if a new rule was made, would it ever be right to . . . steal?"

Papa's heavy dust-colored eyebrows shot up. "I can't imagine why it would be. Although . . . " He turned his head to one side. "I suppose if a Patriot saw an opportunity to steal information from the British to help save lives, that might not be wrong." Papa pressed his lips together for a moment before he went on. "But, no, for the most part, son, I think stealing is wrong."

"But how do you *know?*"

"God," Papa said simply. "His rules never change. If you

follow them, you'll stay on the right path."

Where do I find those rules? Thomas started to ask.

But the parlor door opened, and Mama sailed in with her arms out to Papa, crying, "John!"

Thomas knew his chance was over for now. Maybe later.

"How long will you be here?" Mama said, holding Papa's big hands in her tiny white ones.

"Not long, I'm afraid, my dear," he answered. "I must be in Yorktown when my goods come in. I have to leave this afternoon."

Mama bravely brushed away a tear, and Thomas slipped out of the room.

Alexander arrived a few minutes later, a tan coat flying out behind him as he hurried into the dining room with his bag. Stray strands of honey-colored hair poked out from his ear curls as if he'd put himself together in a hurry.

Thomas tried not to measure his shoulders with his eyes and imagine how he would look in a black cape, but his searching gaze didn't escape Alexander.

"Do I look that bad?" his teacher said, glancing down at his waistcoat and breeches.

"No!" And then before he could stop himself, Thomas said, "Did you have another visit from Xavier Wormeley this morning?"

Alexander looked at him sharply. "How did you know?"

"I . . . I only guessed," Thomas stammered.

"Well, you guessed correctly. Xavier's own horse was stolen yesterday—in the middle of the day while he was dining at Wetherburn's Tavern after church! He was so angry that he nearly dragged Father and me off to the jail without a grain of proof!"

"But it wasn't you!" Thomas cried, and then bit his tongue.

"Of course it wasn't," Alexander said, pawing through his bag, "and I don't want to waste any more breath talking about it. Now, where were we, Thomas? What were we going to learn today?"

"God's laws," Thomas said. Words seemed to be coming out of his mouth as if someone else were controlling them. Those words brought a dimpled grin to Alexander's face.

"Now there's a fine subject," he said. "I think we must include some religion in your education, and it seems you're ready! God's laws, eh? You'll find those in the Bible, of course."

Alexander launched into the lesson as if he'd been preparing all night. "I don't have a Bible with me, but there's time enough for that tomorrow. Let us start with a story. Get comfortable now, Master Hutchinson."

Thomas sprawled his arms on the shiny tabletop and lay his head on them. Alexander leaned back in his chair and started to talk.

"Do you know about Moses?"

Thomas shook his head.

"You're in for a treat," Alexander said.

He told how Moses was assigned by God to get his people out of bondage under the Pharaoh in Egypt and into their own land where they were free to live by God's laws, not the Pharaoh's. God gave Moses everything he needed to make it happen, including parting the Red Sea for the people to get through.

"He would have *had* to do that if I'd been Moses,"

Alexander commented with both dimples engaged. "I can't swim a lick."

He went on to explain that once they reached their "home," God fed the people and provided for them, but they forgot what His laws were and began to behave like heathens.

"It was a lot like those cock fights and wrestling matches they hold behind the taverns sometimes," Alexander said.

Thomas said impatiently, "Go on."

So Alexander told how God sent Moses up to the top of a mountain, where He gave him His laws on large tablets to share with the people.

"There could be no mistake about what God wanted when Moses came down with the Ten Commandments," Alexander said. "We still follow them today. It is, in fact, common law that they be displayed in every church."

"Are they in ours?" Thomas asked.

"Hanging right behind the altar. Along with the Apostle's Creed and the Lord's Prayer."

"That's what those are!" Thomas exclaimed.

"Indeed."

"So," Thomas said, more to himself than to Alexander, "if I follow those, I'm doing what's right."

"By all rights, yes."

Thomas wanted to run to the church right away and read all Ten Commandments, but there was no time before he went to the apothecary shop. And on the way, other thoughts crept into his head.

What if I have to work with Nicholas today? I know I'm supposed to try to find things out from him, but how can I do that? Please, God, don't make me do that today—not until I've had a chance to read the Laws!

It looked as if once again God had answered his prayer. There were several people in the shop, but Nicholas wasn't one of them. Caroline was.

She was pacing up and down in front of the glass-fronted cabinets, pretending to admire the delft blue apothecary jars, but Thomas knew she was doing nothing of the sort. She'd seen those jars almost as many times as he had, and her eyes were now brimming with some kind of news.

He motioned for her to follow him to the back hall. They could talk while he swept.

She started to trail after him, but Francis looked up from the syrup he was pouring and wheezed, "There's no time for that today, Hutchinson! Go to Mistress Wetherburn's and take the leather sling to Dr. Quincy. Cate's got herself a broken arm."

Thomas stared at him in horror.

"Don't stand there gawkin' like a goose!" Francis said, his scalp going crimson. "Go on!"

Thomas grabbed the sling and hurried out the front door with Caroline on his heels.

"Here," she said when they reached the sidewalk. She grabbed his arm and tucked a folded piece of paper into his sleeve. "Read this. It's important!"

There was a tap on the window, and Thomas looked up to see Francis making impatient gestures at him.

"I have to go," Thomas said, backing down the sidewalk. "I'll find you later."

"Read the note," Caroline said over her shoulder as she hurried off the other way. "It's important!"

"I will!"

But as he hurried off toward Mistress Wetherburn's, all Thomas could think about was how he was going to look Nicholas Quincy in the eye.

The note in his sleeve was quickly forgotten.

✝ ✤ ✝

Chapter Fifteen

𝕴t wasn't hard at first to avoid Nicholas's eyes. He was intent on getting Cate's arm into the sling, while she, of course, jabbered on like a mockingbird.

"This never would have happened if it weren't for the mistress!" she told them in a loud whisper, even though they were out in the kitchen building where it was probably impossible for Mistress Wetherburn to hear her.

"She so worried somebody gone take the horses again, she had me in the stables tyin' them to their stalls and one of them horses got spooked and knocked me on the floor." She rolled her big black eyes at Thomas. "As if that thief couldn't untie a knot, even with that mask on."

Thomas could feel his own eyes popping. Cate's got even bigger as she realized she'd said too much.

"How did you know—?" Thomas started to say, and then stopped himself. His eyes shifted uneasily to Nicholas, but Dr. Quincy didn't even seem to be listening. "Did you see the thief?" Thomas finally asked.

"There wasn't nothin' I coulda done to stop him, Master Thomas! He had the biggest arms I ever seen! And mean eyes! Like the devil hisself!"

"What color were his eyes?" Thomas probed. "Could you see that?"

"All right, then, Cate," Nicholas said. "That should mend nicely."

Cate looked at the leather sling in surprise. "You done?"

Nicholas nodded and began to gather up his things.

Cate shook her head in admiration. "My, my. You got the touch of an angel, Dr. Quincy."

"And a good thing he does!" Mistress Wetherburn's shrill voice cut through them all like a newly sharpened knife as she sliced in the kitchen door and stood over Cate with her hands stabbed onto her hips.

Thomas wished she would go away so he could find out from Cate what color the thief's eyes were.

Please, God, he prayed feverishly, *don't let her say brown.*

Mistress Wetherburn's scowl at Cate turned to a generous smile as she looked up at Nicholas.

"As always, you have worked a miracle, Doctor," she oozed.

"God performs the miracles, Mistress Wetherburn," he said. "I merely follow His instructions."

That, however, seemed to pass right over her coifed and curled head. "When will she be able to work? Tomorrow?"

Nicholas looked horrified. "Oh, no, ma'am!" he said. "Not for at least a week. And I must check the arm even then to be sure it's mending."

Mistress Wetherburn glared down at Cate. The slave girl seemed to grow smaller on her pallet right before Thomas's eyes.

"Perhaps in a day or two she can do some light work with her right hand only," Nicholas said, as if he, too, were feeling smaller. "I'm leaving an ointment made from bugle leaf boiled in grease. That should take away the pain and hasten the healing. Give her roasted onion with honey so she can sleep through the pain."

Mistress Wetherburn sighed. "Whatever you say, Doctor. We all must suffer in these times, I suppose."

Thomas was fairly certain she was talking about herself, not Cate. *It's going to be hard for her to get those curls piled up on her head without Cate's two hands*, he thought.

"Let me see you out," she said to Dr. Quincy. They drifted out of the kitchen building with Mistress Wetherburn hanging on his sleeve.

"She'd have my arm chopped off if it meant I could get right up and go back to work!" Cate hissed when they were gone. "She's the devil's woman."

Thomas glanced out the window and then hurried to crouch beside Cate's pallet.

"Do you remember what color the masked thief's eyes were?" he whispered to her.

Without even stopping to think, she nodded her head, and her own eyes swelled in their sockets. "I do, Master Thomas. I'll never forget them."

Thomas could hardly keep from shouting, *Then tell me!*

"They was like Mistress Wetherburn's just now," Cate said. She stared at the kitchen wall as if she were seeing them again at that very moment. "They was the devil's eyes, Master Thomas."

"But what *color?*"

"Why, the devil's color!"

Thomas sank back and sighed heavily. "You mean black—like, brown?"

"No!" Cate said. "Red, Master Thomas. Red!"

"Who in the world has red eyes?" Thomas muttered to himself as he marched, head down, out the Wetherburns' rear gate and down a back lane. Alexander had brown eyes. Nicholas Quincy had almost-blue. Cate couldn't prove that his friends weren't involved in horse thievery. She was too busy seeing the devil in everybody!

At least I didn't have to talk to Nicholas, he thought as he headed for the apothecary shop. *I know Thomas the Tireless is supposed to get information from him, but I can't look him in the eye yet. He'll know right away that I'm hiding something!*

Nicholas was probably still standing on Mistress Wetherburn's front step, listening to her latest list of imaginary ailments. Maybe Thomas could talk Francis into letting him scrub down the cellar, and he wouldn't have to see the doctor for the rest of the day.

"Thomas?" a soft voice said.

Thomas turned and looked up into the pale-blue eyes of Nicholas Quincy.

"Oh!" Thomas said.

Nicholas smiled a half smile. "I'm sorry. I've startled you. I hate to disturb a young man who thinks as deeply as you do."

It crossed Thomas's mind that Nicholas never called him a "boy" like everyone else did. But that thought was quickly replaced by a stab of fear. *What am I going to say now?*

However, it was Nicholas who did the talking. "I never question a man about his private thoughts. Unless I sense that I've offended him in some way. Have I done something wrong, Thomas?"

Thomas could do nothing but stare, lower lip hanging, while his mind raced.

You tell me! Have you? What will happen if I tell you what I saw? I can't! I promised I wouldn't!

"I've caught you unawares," Nicholas said. "Perhaps I can make it easier. I think I know what's bothering you about me."

That didn't make it easier. Thomas wanted to dash into the nearby rose garden and hide himself among the thorns.

"I know what a great Patriot your father is," Nicholas said. "I think you yourself would dash off to the war at once if you were old enough. It is only natural that you would wonder why I don't go and fight for American independence."

Two weeks ago, Thomas would have blurted out, "It's because you're a sissy!" But now he didn't know what to say. He couldn't even move, and Nicholas went on.

"You have become an able assistant to me, and a friend as well. I hope I may consider you a friend."

Thomas managed a nod. His heart was hammering so loudly in his ears that he wondered if Nicholas didn't hear it, too.

"Well, my friend," Nicholas said, "I refuse to fight because I am a Quaker. Our beliefs prevent us from ever raising a hand in anger against another human being."

For a moment, Thomas's heart slowed. "Can't they make you join the army?"

Nicholas smiled faintly. "No. There is freedom of religion

now. Every man is allowed to live as he believes."

The hammering started again. "Then you don't have to follow the Ten Commandments?" Thomas blurted out.

Nicholas cocked his head as he always did when he was puzzled. "Of course I do," he said. "'Thou shalt do no murder' is the sixth commandment. I would give up my own life before I would break it!"

Thomas had never seen such fierceness in the doctor's face. Before he could stop them, dark thoughts crowded into his head. *Then he doesn't believe in the war. He would do anything to stop it . . . even steal horses so that . . . so that . . .*

So that what? Everything was confused and jumbled and upside down again. Tears blurred his eyes, and he could think of only one thing to do.

He ran, stumbling down the cobbled sidewalk with his arms flailing.

"Thomas!" Nicholas called out to him. "Thomas, stop!"

But he didn't, until he reached Francis's cellar, where he clutched his arms around himself and fought back the sobs.

All he could think was, *I want to talk to Caroline.*

That's when he remembered the note she had slipped into his shirt. With fumbling fingers, he dug for it. But it was gone. His sleeve was as empty as the rest of him.

Nicholas didn't come back to the shop that day, and Thomas went through the afternoon with his mind stirring like Esther's butter churn. Francis caught him staring into space so many times that he sent him home before dark.

Caroline wasn't waiting on the corner at Nicholson and North England, nor was she watching for him from her window. He wondered again about the note.

What did she have to tell me that was so important?
Maybe she told Malcolm.

Thomas poked his head into all the Hutchinsons' out-
buildings, but Malcolm wasn't there doing any of his usual
afternoon chores. He went to the stable last, though Malcolm
didn't usually bring Burgess and Musket in from the field this
early.

But when he peered into one of the dark stalls, Malcolm
turned and jumped. Thomas squinted his eyes.

"Why are you grooming Otis's horse?" Thomas asked.

Musket, who looked as old as Otis himself, stood patiently
while Malcolm ran the currycomb across his dull, buff-colored
coat. He was used only to pull the wagon back and forth from
the mill—and to keep Otis company when Esther nagged him
too much. No one had ever taken a brush to his bony hide
that Thomas could remember.

Malcolm crouched down on the other side of Musket, out
of Thomas's sight. "I had nothin' else to do," he said. "The
waitin' is making me restless as a hungry dog."

Something about that didn't settle easily in Thomas's
mind. Malcolm could always find something to do.

"Waiting for what?" Thomas said, crossing to the other
side of Musket so he could see Malcolm's face.

"Information. Did you get any today?"

"No. Only that Cate—that's Mistress Wetherburn's slave
girl—saw the thief with the mask. She said he had big arms."

Malcolm stopped brushing. "Does Alexander Taylor have
big arms?"

"He's strong, but it could have been a dwarf for as much

as we can believe Cate. She also said he had *red* eyes!"

Malcolm gave a disgusted snort. "What of Dr. Quincy?"

"He won't fight in the war because he's a Quaker."

Malcolm cocked a dark eyebrow. "What does that have to do with anythin'?"

"Nothing," Thomas said. "But that's all I found out. Caroline wrote a note to me that she said was important, but I never had a chance to read it before I lost it. Did she tell you what it was about?"

Malcolm shook his head thoughtfully. "I've not seen the lass today," he said, and then his voice faded off to a place as far away as his eyes.

Thomas watched him. He could almost see a plan taking shape in Malcolm's mind.

"Well," Malcolm said finally, "we'll just have to wait and see, won't we?"

"No," said Thomas.

"What do you mean, 'no'? Have you somethin' else in mind?"

"You have. You aren't going to hang about here in the stables and 'wait and see.'" Thomas drove his deep-blue eyes into Malcolm. "Why are you really grooming old Musket?"

Malcolm broke into his boxy smile. "You look just like your father when you do that."

Thomas didn't budge.

"All right," Malcolm said, sighing and tossing the currycomb aside. "But you have to promise not to breathe a word. Or try to stop me."

"Stop you from what?"

Malcolm leaned in close to him. "Tonight, I'm goin' back to the place where we saw the thief leave the horse and

Dr. Quincy pick him up. I'm takin' old Musket because I don't think he'll be missed the way Burgess would be."

"What are you going to do out there?" Thomas asked. His heart was pounding again.

"Watch for the thief and follow him—or Dr. Quincy, if he comes back."

"How will you do that without them seeing you?"

"I have my tricks."

Thomas folded his arms. "What are they? Where did you learn them?"

"I can't tell you."

"Then I can't keep it a secret."

They stared at each other for a long moment before Malcolm shrugged. "If you have to know, my father raised my sister and me because my mother was dead. He made his livin' thievin'. And when I was of age, he taught me. Took me out on most every job."

"Did he steal horses?" Thomas said breathlessly.

"Sometimes."

"Did you ever get caught?"

"Once," Malcolm said casually. "That's why I'm here. The judge said I was too young to spend the rest of my life rottin' in a prison when it hadn't been my choice to steal. So they bound me over as an indentured servant."

Thomas knew he was gaping like an open cellar door, but he was having trouble taking this all in. One thought did take hold, though.

"Is that how you knew the horse was being stolen that first night?"

Malcolm nodded. "And it didn't sound like a professional

thief—not like my father." He looked almost proud. "That's why I think this one will be easy to catch."

"Especially with me along," Thomas said. Where that came from, he couldn't tell. It was just there on his lips when he opened them.

"Ha!"

"You can't stop me! I'll tell them all where you've gone!"

Malcolm's eyes smoldered. "I can get on much better without you, Thomas. I try not to mention it often, but you're a clumsy thing sometimes, though not as bad as you were—"

"I can help! How are you going to follow the masked rider *and* Nicholas at the same time when they're going off in two different directions?"

Malcolm appeared to give that some thought. Thomas prayed silently, *Please, God, let him take me. I have to go!*

"You'll have to follow the masked thief since he's on foot," Malcolm said. "I'm better on a horse, and we'll only have one."

Thomas nodded eagerly and chewed on his nails.

"All right," Malcolm said with a sigh. "But we do it *my* way."

"Of course!"

Malcolm let his face smile. "Good, then, Thomas the Tireless. Meet me here in your darkest clothes at a quarter past 10."

✢ ✦ ✢

Chapter Sixteen

There was no moon that night as the two figures clad in black shirts and breeches led old Musket to the edge of town out Jamestown Road and then climbed on his back. Thomas was tingling all the way from his black woolen cap to the toes of his leather slippers. He was even wearing black knitted stockings—and sweat was seeping from every pore.

"You're gettin' me wet, Tireless," Malcolm said. "Do you have to lean so hard with that sweatin' body?"

Thomas pulled back sheepishly. Malcolm was as cool as if it were mid-November as he guided Musket off the road and into the woods, never ceasing to watch in all directions.

"If you see or hear anything, squeeze my left shoulder," he told Thomas.

Thomas nodded, determined to be the first to detect anything. *He'll find out how valuable I am to have with him*, he assured himself. This was a true adventure, not like the ones he and Caroline had played out on the bridge. For the moment, that made him forget that it was his beloved Nicholas Quincy he was stalking.

To his disappointment, there was nothing to hear before they reached the hiding place. Thomas slid off the horse, and Malcolm led Musket back to a thicket of trees, where he tied him and then crept to catch up. He put his hand up, and Thomas strained to listen.

In a few seconds, he heard hoofbeats pounding evenly on the path. Malcolm put his lips close to Thomas's ear.

"This may not be our masked rider," he said. "The horse sounds too sure of him."

Thomas nodded, but his heart still thundered mightily in his chest. It was all so deliciously dangerous.

Even as they listened, without daring to even peek out from behind the big live oak, the horse slowed and finally stopped in the same spot as before.

"Stay," Malcolm mouthed to Thomas.

Thomas held his breath as Malcolm passed one eye out beyond the tree. As he slid back in, he nodded to Thomas.

"Now?" Thomas said with only a hint of sound.

"Godspeed, Tireless," Malcolm whispered back.

Just as they had agreed, Thomas sneaked out from behind the live oak and watched the masked rider move stealthily into the trees just a little farther up the road. He wasn't running, which meant Thomas didn't have to hurry to catch up with him.

"It's better not to run if you don't have to," Malcolm had advised earlier. "You can walk more quietly."

Thomas didn't miss a step as he followed the thief, being careful to stay in the shadows of the trees as Malcolm had

told him to. He had gone only a short way when he heard
the second set of hoofbeats behind him. Letting the masked
man out of his sight for a split second, Thomas turned to
look.

Maybe it isn't Nicholas this time, he thought desperately.

But the tall, thin man who loped up on his sagging gray
horse was indeed Nicholas Quincy. That, however, was not
what made Thomas gasp out loud.

The horse Nicholas was untying from the tree was the
Hutchinsons' own Burgess.

Malcolm said "*Psst!*" and waved Thomas on impatiently.
With only one more backward glance, Thomas scurried to
make up for lost space.

He picked up the masked rider's trail again within
moments. The man wasn't bothering to stay in the shadows,
and he moved as if he were completely sure that no one
would be out in these woods at this hour to see him.

I see you, you miserable thief, Thomas thought angrily.
*And I'm going to find out who you are and turn you in to
Xavier Wormeley—red eyes and all. You'll wish you had
never been born when that fat magistrate gets hold of you—
and my father, too, for stealing our horse!*

And then he added, *Please, God, don't let it be
Alexander.*

Just then, the masked rider took a turn toward the river,
and Thomas didn't let him out of his sight. It was the best
game he'd ever played, and he wasn't as clumsy as he used to
be. He'd learned a lot from those evenings with Malcolm and
with Caroline, dashing around the Palace Gardens.

Thomas smiled when he thought of Caroline. She didn't

even know that he and Malcolm the Mighty were on this mission. She was going to be so excited when they brought back the identity of the real thief.

Cate was right, Thomas thought as he watched the broad-shouldered man slip easily toward the river. *Even under that cape I can tell he's a big man. He's almost as big as Papa.*

A flood of relief poured through Thomas that made him move even faster. This man was much too big for Alexander's slender build.

Thomas realized that he was getting too close to the thief and dove behind a tree to follow with his eyes and try to catch his breath.

Maybe Tireless isn't such a good name for me, he thought.

The thief stopped, too, and for a moment Thomas was afraid he knew Thomas was behind him. But the man stood on the riverbank, never looking back . . . and then plunged into the water.

Thomas ran to the riverbank, and a memory flashed through his mind. It was Alexander saying, *I can't swim a lick.*

Thomas stopped cold in his tracks and watched the swimmer slice his arms smoothly through the water and disappear into its inky blackness. There was only one person in Williamsburg—perhaps the whole colony of Virginia—who could swim like that.

That was Sam Hutchinson.

It can't be! Thomas wanted to scream out loud. *It can't be!*

Still, he had to find out. He had to swim after him and find out.

Thomas started to kick off his leather slippers when he

heard something behind him that froze his leg in midair.

Was that a scream? he thought wildly. *Was that Malcolm?*

He squeezed his eyes shut to listen. There was no other sound, except the frightened whinnying of a horse. Thomas knew that sound for sure. It was old Musket.

Thomas turned again toward the river, but there was neither sight nor sound of . . . the swimmer. Thomas still couldn't bring himself to think that it had really been Sam. Now he couldn't find out anyway. He was probably all the way to the other bank by now, and Thomas knew he could never catch him, whoever he was. He turned back toward the woods.

"Malcolm!" he called out in a hoarse whisper. "Malcolm, are you all right?"

His only answer was a moan that came all the way up from someone's soul.

Not worrying about shadows this time, Thomas tore through the woods with his heart lodged in his throat. If that had been Malcolm, he was hurt—badly hurt.

He whipped past the spot where they'd hidden and then beyond the thicket where Musket had been tied. He found them both on the path several strides farther. Musket was just struggling to stand up. Malcolm, on the ground, wasn't moving at all.

Thomas flung himself down beside him and put his face close to his friend's.

"Malcolm!" he shouted. "Malcolm, talk to me!"

But nothing came out of Malcolm's mouth except a trail of blood to match the two that trickled from his nose. Even in the dark, Thomas could see that his face was bluish-white and that he was fighting to breathe.

"No!" Thomas cried.

He pulled Malcolm's shoulders up in his arms and cradled his head against his chest. Air burst from Malcolm's mouth and rattled in his chest. Thomas held him there and looked around frantically.

"What do I do now, Malcolm?" he said, sobbing now. "You didn't tell me what to do if this happened! I need help!"

Help. Of course. Thomas chomped down on the inside of his mouth and tried to get control of his runaway thoughts. *Who can I go to? Papa isn't home. Nicholas . . . Old Francis . . . he'll know what to do.*

Thomas looked down at Malcolm's lifeless face and said to him, "I'm going to leave you here, Mighty, but only for as long as it takes me to get to Williamsburg and rouse Francis. I'll bring him back, I promise."

He suddenly cut off his words and listened. More hoof-beats—coming from the other direction—down toward the Digges's plantation. Thomas lowered his head onto Malcolm and held his breath.

The horse drew closer and then stopped . . . right about where the masked rider had left Burgess tied. Thomas could hear the horse's hooves prancing as if the rider didn't want to stay long. And then the horse took off at a gallop, back the way it had come.

That was the other thief, Thomas told himself, as surely as if he were reciting the multiplication tables. He came to pick up Burgess—and didn't find him where he expected to. *But that doesn't make sense! What about Nicholas?*

Thomas lowered Malcolm gently so that his head rested against a rock. He seemed to breathe more easily when he was propped up. Thomas smeared the tears from his face and said, "I'm going for help."

He started to stand, but a hand held him lightly by the shoulder.

"There's no need to do that," someone said. "I'm here."

Thomas felt as if he were paralyzed. It was Nicholas Quincy.

Before Thomas could shout or scream or even take off running, Nicholas had gently pushed him out of the way and was bending over Malcolm.

"Good work, Thomas," he said as he loosened Malcolm's clothing and ran his hands tenderly down his legs and arms. "Keeping his head up like that kept him breathing. You probably saved his life."

"What are you going to do?" Thomas burst out.

"Whatever I can." His lips tightened into a grim line. "But I can't do much of it out here, and I'm afraid to try to take him back on horseback. We'll need a wagon." He looked up at Thomas. "Will you ride back into town and fetch one? I think I can keep him hanging on until you get back. God willing."

For a moment, Thomas could only stare at him. Was this the same man who only minutes before had stolen the Hutchinsons' horse?

"Where's Burgess?" Thomas cried.

"I don't know who Burgess is," Nicholas said quietly. "But I need a wagon, Thomas. I need it soon."

"Is he going to die?" Thomas asked. He knew he wasn't making sense, but nothing made sense anymore. Nothing.

"Not if you bring help."

It was the first time Thomas had ever heard even a trace

of anything stern in Nicholas's voice. It seemed to crack at him like a whip, and Thomas bolted toward Musket.

"I'll be back!" he shouted as he scrambled onto the old horse's back. "I'll be back with a wagon!"

Thomas had never ridden as hard as he did down Jamestown Road to Williamsburg, especially on a bony old horse who heaved and wheezed worse than Francis Pickering.

And he had never prayed as hard either. *God, please let me get back in time with the wagon,* he kept saying over and over. *Please don't let Malcolm die. Please!*

Drenched with sweat and tears, he finally rode into the Hutchinson yard, where Otis was standing, bewildered, outside the stable in his nightshift. Malcolm had been wrong when he'd said Burgess would be missed first.

"Hitch Musket up to the wagon!" Thomas shouted as he slid from the old horse's back. "Malcolm's hurt in the woods, and Nicholas Quincy says he can only bring him back in a wagon—or he'll die!"

"So will this horse," Otis said. "He'll drop if he takes one more step. Look, his leg's near broke from a fall. I don't know how he made it this far."

"But what about Malcolm?" Thomas screamed at him. "I can't let him die!"

"What is it, Thomas?"

Then another voice joined in. "What is all this about?"

Mama's white-capped head had appeared in the upstairs window just as Esther stalked out of the servants' quarters with a blanket wrapped around her nightgown.

"I need a wagon to get Malcolm! He's hurt in the woods with Dr. Quincy!"

Thomas felt as if he'd said it a thousand times, and still no one would help him.

"What in the name of Beelzebub is Malcolm doing in the woods at this time of night?" Esther asked.

"Thomas, what is it you're saying?" Mama called down.

"A wagon! I need a wagon!"

Thomas burst into fresh sobs. It was then that Otis took him by the arm and led him from the yard.

"We'll use the Taylors' horses," he said over his shoulder. "Get a bed ready for Malcolm."

Thomas stopped crying and stared up at Otis as the old man hauled him down Scotland Street toward North England. There was one thing about not talking much—you must hear more of what other people are saying.

Both Otis and Thomas pounded on the Taylors' front door until it opened a crack. Thomas found himself nose-to-nose with the barrel of a pistol.

"It's me, sir!" Thomas cried out. "Thomas Hutchinson!"

A flustered Robert Taylor flung the door open wide and brought down the gun. "Thomas, I'm sorry. I thought you were Xavier Wormeley. What on earth are you doing here?"

For the thousand and first time, Thomas explained. Before he could even finish, Robert was throwing off the banian robe he wore over his nightclothes and saying, "Meet me in the stables. We can be on our way posthaste."

Thomas hurried through the hall to the back door with the first ray of hope shining in his mind. The second ray met him at the back door. Caroline grabbed at his sleeve.

"Are you all right, Thomas?"

"Yes! But Malcolm isn't!"

"I heard." She gathered a pink shawl around her shoulders. "Do you need any medicine?"

Thomas hadn't thought of that. Dr. Quincy could start taking care of Malcolm on the way back.

"Have you any hartshorn?" Thomas said. "And soapwort?"

"We have everything!" she said. "You know how sick Mama gets—"

"Get them!" Thomas said. "I'm leaving in the wagon with your papa!"

Just as Robert Taylor got his horse hitched up to the wagon and he and Thomas were climbing in, Caroline raced across the yard wearing a cape and carrying a bundle, which she handed up to Thomas.

"Do you know where there are any blankets, Papa?" she asked. "Dr. Quincy might need them."

Robert Taylor nodded and went back into the stable.

"Good-bye, Caroline," Thomas said.

But to his astonishment, she climbed deftly over the wheel and curled up under the seat in the wagon.

"What are you doing?" Thomas hissed to her.

"I'm going with you," she hissed back. "Now hush up and don't tell, or I'll never forgive you!"

Thomas hushed. He had no intention of telling.

✜ ✜ ✜

Chapter Seventeen

𝕴t seemed to take hours to get back to the spot where Malcolm lay. Thomas had to clamp down his lip to keep from pleading with Caroline's father to drive the horse on faster.

"Here!" he cried out when they reached the place where the path veered off from Jamestown Road.

"I can't take a wagon down that, son," Robert said. "We'll have to carry him out."

Thomas sailed from the seat and was halfway there before he heard Robert even start down the path.

Behind him, he caught the surprised words, "Caroline! What on earth—?" But that was all.

Nicholas was there when Thomas stumbled to the spot. He was still cradling Malcolm's head in his arms, but the black eyes were closed and the face was gray.

"Amen," Nicholas whispered softly.

He looked up at Thomas.

"We've brought a wagon . . . and some hartshorn . . . and

some soapwort . . . and some blankets. . . ."

Thomas gasped for a breath, and Nicholas murmured, "Thank the Lord."

"Is he . . . dead?" Caroline whispered at his side.

No one answered. From the way Nicholas and Robert hustled to put Malcolm in a blanket sling and get him to the wagon, they could guess that he was still alive, but barely.

"I must ride in back with him," Nicholas said when they had Malcolm bundled in. "I'll try the hartshorn now." He looked down at Thomas and Caroline with troubled eyes. "Would you take Dolly back to town? Thomas, your horse is tied off the road, just over that way." He pointed then added, "You'll want to ride him back, I know."

Thomas could feel his jaw dropping—and the old anger suddenly clawing at his neck.

"I can explain," Nicholas said. His pale eyes were moist. "And I will—later."

"Follow closely," Robert said to Caroline, his eyes sharp.

"Yes, Papa," she said obediently.

Thomas was still rooted to the ground when the wagon lurched away, and Caroline had to take him by the arm and lead him to Dolly.

"There, there, girl," she said.

The horse nuzzled her neck and let her climb on without a whinny.

"Come on, Thomas. We'll ride to where Burgess is."

"He stole our horse," Thomas said, staring after the wagon. He started to cry again—big, silent tears. "He stole our horse."

"I know, Tom," Caroline whispered. "Let's go home, now."

They found a jittery Burgess not far away, and Caroline

calmed him while Thomas mounted. The tears were still streaming from his eyes as they picked their way back to the road and caught up with the wagon. As they followed from a distance, they could see Nicholas silhouetted by the lantern Robert had up front with him. The doctor appeared to be working on Malcolm.

"You see, he's still alive," Caroline said.

Thomas nodded and swiped at his tears.

They rode in silence for a while until Caroline said in a careful voice, "Did you see Sam, then, Tom?"

Thomas jerked in the saddle. "Sam? How did you know—?" He stopped and set his jaw. "I don't know what you're talking about. I didn't see Sam."

"Yes, you did," Caroline said gently. "I can tell."

Thomas ran a panicky hand through his hair. The woolen cap had long since fallen off. "Was it really Sam, then, Caroline?" he said tearfully. "How do you know?"

"Didn't you read my note?"

Thomas shook his head miserably. "I lost it before I had a chance to."

Caroline's brown eyes sprang open in alarm. "I hope no one else finds it and reads it!"

"Why?"

"Because it says that Sam is the thief!"

"But how do you know?"

Caroline looked down at the reins she was holding. "I read Alexander's journal. I couldn't stand it a moment longer, Tom! Even though I kept saying I knew it wasn't Alexander, there was this terrible little voice inside my head that kept saying, *But maybe it is! What if it is?* He writes everything in his journal, he told me once. So while he was with you at lessons, I slipped into his room and read it."

Thomas felt a sinking feeling of dread. "What did it say?"

"It said that he has been spending his afternoons and even some nights hiding at the college, listening to the boys talk. Papa has been doing the same thing in the taverns! They thought they might hear someone making plans . . . and they did." She looked mournfully at Thomas. "I'm sorry, Tom. I know what it feels like to think that your brother has done something bad."

She couldn't know how he felt. She couldn't know what it was like to feel as if you were going to die because something was pressing so hard against your chest.

Caroline sighed as if she would rather throw herself from the horse than say it. "He heard Sam and Ulysses Digges and some of the other Patriot boys saying how they had been stealing Patriots' horses and hiding them in a back acre of Peyton Digges's plantation while he was in bed with the fever."

"Why would they do that?"

"To make it look as if the Loyalists were doing it. That way, since your father won't let Xavier Wormeley drive the Loyalists out of town, he could just hang them!"

"Sam wouldn't do that!"

"He did, Tom. The boys said they stopped for a while because when they took Isaiah Chowning's horse, it got away and found its way back home, and they had to be careful not to make any more mistakes or they'd be caught." Caroline looked at him sideways. "So did you see Sam?"

"I saw someone with big arms like him who could swim

like him," Thomas said fiercely, "but I couldn't see him! The man was wearing a mask!" He turned to Caroline with the tears streaming again. "But we saw Nicholas! He wasn't wearing a mask! Let them put him in jail!"

Caroline was quiet for a while. The only sounds were the rocking of the wagon far ahead of them, and the squeaking of the leather on their mounts. Finally, she said, "I don't think you want that either, Tom. You love Nicholas almost as much as you do Sam . . . or Alexander . . . or Malcolm."

That was true, and Thomas knew it. But he also knew that none of them had followed God's rules, and right now, every one of those people he loved was in deep, deep trouble.

When they reached the Hutchinson yard, Otis opened the double gates, and Esther and Mama led the way up to Thomas's room, where Malcolm was laid on clean sheets that smelled of lavender. Nicholas murmured a thank you and then ignored them all as he bent over the boy and went to work.

Somewhere in the background, Mama thanked Robert Taylor with tears in her voice, and Robert packed Caroline off for home. Esther heated water and Mama brought pan after pan of it up the stairs, only to leave moments later with another pan filled with blood.

No one questioned what Thomas was doing or tried to send him to bed. They left him alone to stand beside Nicholas, cleaning Malcolm's wounds, putting medicine to his lips, and begging God not to let him die.

At dawn, Malcolm still had not opened his eyes, and Thomas put his face in his arms on the side of the bed in despair.

"Where are you, God?" he sobbed. "Why don't you wake him up?"

"He's here," a gentle voice said beside him. "Perhaps He only wants him to sleep."

Then the room fell silent. God obviously wanted Thomas to sleep, too, because he awoke with a start hours later.

Malcolm was still breathing noisily, and Nicholas was sitting in a chair on the other side of the bed, watching Malcolm's face and moving his lips.

Thomas stumbled to his feet. "Did he wake up?"

"Not yet. He must have hit his head hard when he fell off his horse. It may be a while."

Thomas reached for a cloth to wipe Malcolm's forehead, but Nicholas said, "Why don't you go down and eat some breakfast? You need strength if you're going to help Malcolm."

"Breakfast?" Thomas said suddenly. "I have to do the chores today!"

He staggered down the stairs in a fog and was only dimly aware of how hot he was in the black breeches and shirt and heavy wool stockings he was still wearing. There was wood to chop and water to fetch. . . .

But when he reached the wood pile, someone else was already there—sleeves rolled up, swinging the wooden club into the wedge he'd placed in a log, sweat rolling down his forehead from his honey-colored hair.

"Alexander!" Thomas said.

Alexander stopped and rested on the club handle and tried to smile. But he looked as unhappy as Thomas felt.

"Good morning," he said sadly. "I thought I'd take care of some of this work for you and Malcolm. How is he?"

"The same," Thomas said. And then he felt as if he were cracking open like an egg. "Is it true, then?" he said through a new set of tears.

Alexander put down the club and sat on the log. He stared down at his hands for a long time before he said, "I'm afraid it is, Thomas. I never expected to find Sam guilty. I only wanted to find a way to prove my own innocence, and my father's. I hope you understand."

Thomas wasn't sure he understood anything, but he nodded.

"Father and I have agreed not to say anything until your papa gets home. He'll know what to do about Sam."

"Papa?" Thomas cried. "Does he have to know?"

A pain crossed Alexander's face. "If he doesn't, then sooner or later Xavier Wormeley will find a way to 'prove' that it was we who did it. I can't hang for something I didn't do."

Thomas could feel the horror in his own eyes. "Hang?" he said. He could hardly hear his own voice. "Sam will hang, then?"

Alexander stood up and put both hands on Thomas's shoulders. "I don't think Sam will hang. Your father will know what to do. I would be happy to go to Yorktown and bring him back here. Would you like for me to do that?"

"Will you tell him?"

"Not if you don't want me to. I'm sure he'll come if I simply tell him you need him. You are his pride and joy, Thomas."

"I am?" Thomas said.

A tiny pinpoint of light was shining somewhere in the back of his head. When Alexander nodded and said "He told me so once," the light got a little bigger.

As Alexander picked up the club to finish the wood-cutting, Thomas remembered something.

"What about Nicholas?" he asked.

"The doctor? What of him?"

"You don't know about him, stealing with Sam?"

Alexander shook his head and went back to chopping. "No one ever mentioned his name," he said. "I'll leave for Yorktown as soon as I've finished here."

More confused than ever, Thomas wandered into the kitchen building, but Esther was fast asleep in the chair by the window, snoring in funny little puffs. Beside her was the water barrel. She'd been to the well herself.

Thomas decided he wasn't hungry anyway and made his way back up the stairs. He was a few steps away from the closed door when he heard wailing from inside. It was Mama crying, "Oh, dear! Oh, dear!" Nicholas was praying and Mama was wailing—and there was no sound of rattled breathing.

"No!" Thomas cried.

The hall and the stairs and the front door all blurred before him as he tore from the house and across the Palace Green, crying, "No! Malcolm, no!"

He didn't stop until he reached the college, and then he pawed his way to Sam's room hiccuping and letting the anger singe all the way up his backbone to his brain.

When his brother opened the door to him, Thomas lunged at him with his fists flying.

"Malcolm is dead!" he screamed. "And you killed him!"

⁜ ⁜ ⁜

Chapter Eighteen

During the first moment of surprise, Sam didn't move. But when Thomas landed a punch on his jaw, Sam wrestled him to the floor and held him down with both hands. Thomas kicked and strained until Sam said harshly, "Stop it!"

Thomas immediately crumpled into tears and ripped his arms away.

"Are you going to come at me again?" Sam asked.

Thomas shook his head miserably.

"Then I'll let you up."

Sam stood and put a hand down to help his brother, but Thomas shoved it aside and got to his feet himself. He raked his arm across his face and forced himself to stop crying.

"Now," Sam said, facing him with his hands on his hips. "What is this about me killing someone?"

"Malcolm!" Thomas said, and sniffed loudly. "He fell off his horse last night and now he's dead! Not even Nicholas could save him."

Sam's brow furrowed. "I'm sorry to hear it, Thomas, truly I am. But what have I to do with that?"

"It happened when we were following—"

Thomas stopped. In spite of the anger that flared through every part of him, he wasn't sure he could say it.

"Following who? Thomas, you are making no sense."

"Following you!"

Silence fell like a club to a wedge, and understanding spread over Sam's face.

"Where?" he said in a wooden voice. "When?"

"Last night. Off Jamestown Road. When you were delivering the stolen horse—*our* horse!"

Sam turned from him and ran a hand down the back of his blond hair.

Thomas watched his broad back and then closed his eyes. He didn't want to imagine it in a black cape.

When Sam turned around, his face was soft. "I understand your grief, Thomas. You're looking for someone to blame. But I'm not responsible. I was here last night, studying natural philosophy—"

"You weren't!"

"They keep us locked in here at night! How would I get out?"

"I don't know!" Thomas was shouting now. "But I saw you tie Burgess to a tree, and I followed you through the woods. I watched you jump into the river and swim away!"

Sam blinked, but only for a second. Thomas watched with a flicker of fear as Sam's blue eyes grew cold. "But you didn't see my face, did you, Thomas?"

Thomas stared.

"Did you?"

"No," Thomas said faintly. "You were wearing a mask."

Sam exploded into a laugh. "You've been playing too many games in the Palace Gardens with that little Loyalist friend of yours!" he cried. "You've completely let her take your imagination and run away with it. Why would I steal my own horse?"

"I don't know, but Alexander heard you and Ulysses and the others talking—"

"And you believe that stinking Loyalist over me?"

Sam brought his face close to Thomas's and waited. It was Thomas's turn to blink.

"He wrote it in his journal," he said weakly.

"What does that prove?"

Thomas's head was spinning. *What does it prove? Who am I to believe? God, please tell me who to believe!*

Sam put his hand on Thomas's shoulder and squeezed it. "I am not angry with you for accusing me, Thomas. When someone you love dies, you want someone to blame. I'm flattered that you think I'm strong enough to take it."

He flashed his smile, and the fear drained out of Thomas. That was it. It had to be. What did he really know for sure?

"I want to believe you, Sam."

"Then do. You can, you know—"

He was interrupted by a knock on the door. Before he could answer, Ulysses Digges stuck his head in the room. As usual, his eyes passed over Thomas as if he weren't there. He stepped in and stuck a pile of what looked like damp rags out to Sam.

"Here are your wet clothes," he said. "I don't want the old Sour Face finding them hanging up in my room."

Sam snatched them from him and said gruffly, "Thank you."

"The mask will dry, but I don't know about the cape. Why do you always have to jump in the river, show-off?"

"Thank you!" Sam said with pointed eyes. He nodded toward Thomas, and Ulysses gasped as if he were seeing him for the first time. He wasn't out of the room before the floor started to cave in under Thomas's feet.

He grabbed the wet clothes from Sam and tore into them. They fell to the ground until Thomas had only a damp black mask and a soaked black cape in his hands. He looked at Sam with tears burning his eyes.

"That's where you had been that night at the bridge. You had just stolen Mister Wetherburn's horse and then—"

"You don't understand, Thomas," Sam said sternly.

"Don't give me a lecture!" Thomas screamed at him. "You stole, and that's wrong! You were going to let someone else hang for it, and that's wrong! What about the rules, Sam?"

"I wasn't going to let them hang! I just wanted them to leave Williamsburg! And besides, the rules are changing. We're fighting a war to change the rules, but we can't win it unless we get rid of the people who are against us. When you grow up, Thomas—"

"I am grown up—"

"—*when* you grow up, you will realize that sometimes you have to do drastic things to change the rules. Men are leaving their homes and marching barefoot in snow and even dying so the rules can change. Father won't allow me to go and join them, so I have to do what I can here."

"God's rules can't be changed," Thomas said.

Sam frowned. "What?"

"Some things are just wrong, no matter what. You can't change God's rules."

Slowly, Sam folded his arms across his chest. "What are you going to do?"

Thomas swallowed hard. "I don't know. Papa's coming back today."

"Are you going to tell him?"

Thomas couldn't answer.

Sam watched his face carefully. Then, eyes slanting slyly, he reached out and took the cape and draped it around Thomas's shoulders. The dampness of it, and the look in Sam's eyes, sent a chill through Thomas. A thought sprang uninvited into his head: *No wonder Cate thought you had eyes like the devil.*

"What are you doing?" Thomas asked.

"You look masterful in it, I must admit," Sam said.

"What are you talking about?"

"How would you like to be partners with Ulysses and me and the others?"

"Partners?"

"You know how the scheme works now. Why don't you join us? You're brave, you're smart." Sam clapped him on the shoulder. "You're still a bit clumsy, but I'm sure we can train you. . . ."

His voice drifted off as Thomas let the wet cape drop from his back and stared hard at his brother. So many times he had longed to be included by Sam and his friends. Now it was happening—and only so he wouldn't tell his father what they were doing. Suddenly, Thomas was so tired that he wasn't sure he could even walk to the door.

But with heavy legs and a heavier heart, he did. Sam called to him once, but he didn't stop. He wandered up the Duke of Gloucester Street with the thoughts falling like pieces of lead into his mind.

I talk about God's laws never changing, and I pray, and I believe . . . but what good does it do me? said one thought.

Why don't I just go back to being angry and beating people up? said another.

Is there anyone I can trust anymore—anyone who can answer my questions?

Papa is never here.

Sam is a thief and a murderer.

Alexander will have to leave Williamsburg if he's to keep his life, since everyone thinks he's guilty.

Malcolm is gone.

And Nicholas . . .

Thomas couldn't walk anymore, and he sank onto a set of steps and hung his head in his arms. Behind him, a door opened. Someone sat down beside him with a wheezing breath and put a bony old hand on his shoulder.

"I didn't expect to see you here today, young Hutchinson," Francis said. "Not after all you've been through."

Thomas lifted his head and realized he was sitting in front of the apothecary shop. The smell of ginger and cinnamon wafted out and mingled with the July heat, making Thomas want to cry again. Only there were no more tears left. He felt as if there were nothing left inside him at all.

"I don't think I can sweep today, sir," he said. "I'm too tired."

"Come inside, then," Francis said in his raspy voice. "I think a cup of bee balm tea is what you need."

Thomas dragged himself inside the shop and followed Francis into the examining room. He was about to drop into a chair when he saw a figure fast asleep with his head on Francis's desk.

"Someone else is in need of bee balm as well," Francis said. "He'll be grateful for your company."

Thomas wanted to bolt from the room. He didn't want to hear any more of the people he'd once admired trying to explain why they'd broken the rules—and broken his heart.

But his legs wouldn't move, and he stayed in the chair and took the hot cup Francis put in his hand. The apothecary moved to the figure at his desk. "Here's your tea, Doctor," the old man said, nudging him with a finger.

Nicholas lifted his head and smiled sleepily. Francis walked stiffly from the room like an old owl. Thomas stared into his tea cup.

"I think it's time I explained," Nicholas said when he saw him.

Thomas didn't answer, and he didn't look up. He heard Nicholas get up from his chair and perch on the edge of the desk near him. "Do you remember the night you went with me to the Digges's plantation?" the doctor asked.

Thomas nodded numbly.

"That was the night I think we became friends," Nicholas said. "And it was also the night we became enemies."

Thomas's mind whirled dizzily. He still said nothing.

"That night, when you went downstairs with Mistress Digges, Peyton told me that he'd heard his son Ulysses and your brother Sam talking when they thought he was unconscious with fever. They agreed that they would hide the horses they were taking in a back acre of his plantation until the Loyalists had all left town. Then they would return them to their owners. They didn't think he would ever know, since he was so ill. By the time he recovered, the horses would be safely back in their own stables." Nicholas put his hand to his chest as if he felt Peyton Digges's pain. "The poor man didn't know whom to turn to, so I promised I would help him."

Thomas felt as if he were slowly waking up from a nightmare. "How? How could you help him?"

"I visited him every day to see if he had heard them talking again. The next time he heard that they planned to steal another horse, he told me, and I followed Sam and took the horse before Ulysses could get there, and I returned it."

"To Isaiah Chowning," Thomas said.

Nicholas nodded. "I thought that had cured them, because they didn't steal again for a long time. I was happy about that. Ulysses Digges was one of my first patients when I came here, although little did I know that the hand I was bandaging had been cut in an act of thievery. And then there are you and Caroline. It would give me great pain to see you and your families hurt."

There was a mist in Nicholas's eyes, and Thomas looked away so he wouldn't start to cry again. There were tears left inside him after all.

"Then you aren't a thief?" Thomas asked.

"No."

"We thought you were when we saw you on Sunday, me and Caroline and—"

Thomas's voice broke, and he hung his head and let the tears fall. "Malcolm was only trying to help, too. Why did he have to die?"

"Die?"

Thomas nodded and cried. At once, Nicholas was at his side, lifting his chin.

"Thomas!" he said. "Did you think Malcolm was dead?"

"Yes! I heard Mama wailing and you praying, and I couldn't hear Malcolm breathing anymore. That's how I knew."

Nicholas let his head fall back and laughed softly toward the ceiling. "Oh, no, Thomas," he said. "Those were tears of joy and prayers of thanks and the sweet, quiet breath of life. Malcolm isn't dead! He's going to be all right. He's going to be fine!"

Thomas jumped up and knocked over the chair behind him.

"Alive?" he said.

"Alive and awake. And asking to see you. But you ran off before anyone could catch you!"

"I'll go now!"

He charged toward the door.

"Thomas, there's something else," Nicholas said.

Something in his voice stopped Thomas in the doorway. He turned to find Nicholas holding out a piece of paper.

"You dropped this when we were talking yesterday. I want to give it back to you, because I don't think anyone else should find it and read it."

Thomas knew what it was right away—the note from Caroline telling all about Sam. He didn't even want to touch it.

"Burn it, sir," Thomas said. "Can we go see Malcolm now?"

Nicholas nodded and crumpled the note in his fist. The two of them passed into the front of the shop.

Francis was standing at the window, and he turned and put his hand up for them to be quiet.

"What is it, Francis?" Nicholas asked.

"Xavier Wormeley is at it again," Francis said bitterly. "Alexander Taylor just rode into town with John Hutchinson, and Xavier and Peter Pelham flagged the boy down. They're puttin' him in the jailer's wagon now."

"No!" Thomas shouted.

He flung open the front door and met his father's eyes as he flew down the steps.

"Get Robert Taylor," he heard Francis hiss to Nicholas as the door slammed behind him.

"No!" Thomas cried again. "Alexander didn't do it! He didn't steal the horses!"

"Call your boy off, Hutchinson," Xavier said with puffed-up importance. He stood leaning against the wagon while Peter Pelham tied Alexander's hands behind his back. Alexander held his honey-colored head high, but his face was ashen and pinched with fear.

"Why should I, Xavier?" Papa said, his eyes throwing daggers at the magistrate. "I agree with him! What proof could you possibly have that this young man is guilty of thievery?"

"That is for the court to hear," Xavier said, smacking his thick lips together. And then like a bully who can't resist showing off, he added, "But I will say this, Hutchinson. I have a witness."

Papa's eyebrows went up slowly. "What witness?"

Thomas crept to his side to listen.

"Mistress Wetherburn's slave girl. I've talked to her myself. She was talking in her sleep about a masked thief stealing the horse, and of course Mistress Wetherburn summoned me at once."

"Of course," Papa said. His voice was reining in anger.

"The girl admitted that she saw the thief herself," Xavier went on, wagging his head. "She said he was young and strong." He nodded toward Alexander.

"And *that's* your proof?" Papa gave a hard laugh. "You'd best let the young man go now, before the court has you hanged for making a false accusation!"

"I beg your pardon, Mr. Hutchinson! How dare you question my judgment?"

Thomas could hold back no longer. "Because she's so afraid of you, she would say anything! She didn't see his face! He was wearing a mask!"

All eyes turned to Thomas. He put his hand over his mouth, but the words had already escaped, and there was no pulling them back now.

"That is beside the point!" Xavier cried, his face going scarlet down to his jowls.

"That is *entirely* the point if the thief was indeed wearing a mask!" Papa said. His eyes lingered on Thomas for a moment as if he were storing a question away for later.

Xavier coughed and harrumphed and waggled his jowls like a turkey while everyone watched. His eyes, too, lit on Thomas, and something sparked in the tiny poke holes.

"How did you know the thief was wearing a mask, boy?"

For a fleeting moment, Thomas wanted to say that Cate had told him. It would all be so easy. . . .

But only for me, he thought. Cate would probably get the whipping of her life for not telling Mistress Wetherburn sooner!

"Well?" Xavier said, foot tapping.

"Tell the truth, Thomas," Papa said quietly. "A Hutchinson always tells the truth."

"I saw him, too," Thomas said. "And I know it wasn't Alexander Taylor. He was too tall and too broad-shouldered to be him—"

Thomas stopped. Surely, he'd said enough.

But Xavier pulled away from the wagon and came toward him, jabbing a sausage finger. "You'll say anything to protect your Loyalist friends, boy! The only way you'll ever convince me that it was not this miserable creature wearing that mask is to tell me who it was!" His face was so close that Thomas could smell the salt pork on his breath. "If you know who it is, boy, why don't you tell us all?"

✞ ✛ ✞

Chapter Nineteen

Thomas looked frantically at his father.

"If you know, Thomas, then tell the man," Papa said. "It could mean Alexander's life."

Then another voice joined the fray. "What is the meaning of this?"

It was Robert Taylor, calling from the corner. He marched toward the group with his fists doubled. "Untie my son at once, Wormeley! This has gone far enough!"

He walked up to Alexander and grabbed his arm away from Peter Pelham.

"Arrest this man!" Xavier cried out, gleefully. "They were working together, I'm sure of it!"

"Xavier, have you lost your mind?" John Hutchinson said.

But the magistrate ignored him as he dusted his hands together and waddled off toward the courthouse. "I have preparations to make!" he said over his shoulder. "There must be a speedy trial!"

They watched him go, and they watched Peter Pelham

drive off toward the jail with Alexander and Robert bound in the back.

"Don't worry!" Papa called after them. "I shall sort this out and have you back at home in no time!"

But the face that watched them disappear behind the empty Capitol Building was starched with concern. He looked down at Thomas and said, "Let us go home, son."

Thomas rode behind his father on Judge. Neither of them spoke until they entered the parlor and greeted Mama. Papa asked for citron water all around and told Thomas to sit down.

I want to go up and see Malcolm! Thomas cried inside. *I want to change from these hot clothes I have been wearing since last night! I want to do anything but stay here and answer these questions! I can't do it!*

But he sat down, and he waited.

"I would like to help the Taylors," his father said when Esther had served their drinks in cool goblets and left the room. "They have been good neighbors to us, and I do not want to see them punished unjustly."

"No," Thomas said faintly. His heart was beating so hard it hurt.

"But I cannot help them unless I know everything. Can you help me, Thomas?"

Slowly, Thomas nodded.

"What is it, John?" Mama said. "What's happened?"

"Young Alexander Taylor arrived at the Homestead this morning and insisted I come to Williamsburg because Thomas needed my help."

"Why, Thomas!" Mama started to say, but Papa covered her hand with his.

"When Alexander and I arrived, Xavier Wormeley was there to arrest the young man for horse theft. As you can imagine, a muddle followed."

"Of course," said Mama, clenching her tiny white hands into two pink balls.

"But I think I am making some sense of it now." He looked directly at Thomas with his piercing blue eyes. The solemn brows were twisted together, but it wasn't The Look. It was a clear request for the truth. "I think Thomas knows who the real thief is, and I think he needs my help in letting it go. Is that right, Thomas?"

Thomas felt his chest explode. "Yes, Papa! I can't do it alone! I don't know which rules to follow!"

Papa nodded and stood up.

I have no choice now, Thomas thought sadly. *He's going to make me tell.*

But to his surprise, Papa said, "Shall we all bow our heads?"

Three heads went down and three pairs of hands folded in front of three anxious hearts. And Papa began to pray.

"Father, we come before You with souls burdened with grief. Your son Thomas has a difficult decision to make, and it has brought pain to us all. We ask that You guide him in following Your laws and only Yours, and that You will guide us, his parents, to uphold him if by chance his heart should break. This we beg for Jesus Christ's sake. Amen."

Thomas didn't open his eyes or lift his head for a long time. He just wanted Papa's words to stay wrapped around him for a little longer—before he had to look at him and say, "Papa, it was your son who stole the horses. It was Sam."

Another thought came to him as he sat with his eyelids trembling. If he didn't tell Papa, surely Nicholas would. He had worked too hard to protect Alexander to let him hang now. And certainly Alexander himself wouldn't go to his grave with Sam's secret in his heart. Even if he thought no one would believe him, wouldn't he at least try?

Thomas shivered. He didn't want his father to hear this news from anyone else. If he had to be disappointed for the rest of his life, let it be right here in this room with only him and Mama and no one else to see his shame.

As Thomas raised his head, the front door opened and closed, and footsteps tapped across the pine floor of the hall and into the parlor. Sam's broad shoulders filled the doorway.

"Thomas, have you told him?" he said. His breath came out in huge gasps as if he'd run all the way from the college.

Thomas shook his head.

"You don't have to," Sam said.

Thomas searched Sam's face with his heart battering his chest. The devil eyes were gone. There were tears there now, and pain like the pain Thomas could feel pressing inside him.

"I'm going to tell him myself," Sam said. He took one more breath and looked at John Hutchinson. "I beg your forgiveness, Father. But I've done something very, very wrong."

And so they sat there—Papa, Mama, and Thomas—while Sam poured out his story with fear in his voice and tears rolling down his handsome face. The whole tale unfolded....

How he and Ulysses had talked about how clever a scheme it would be to steal Patriots' horses and hide them until Xavier had made the Loyalists' lives so miserable that they would leave town—but how they had never actually planned to do it.

How angry he had been that night at dinner when Papa said he would not allow him to go to war.

How he'd run back to the college and said to Ulysses, "Let's do it now, before I lose my nerve. I have to do something to help the war, even if it is only driving the Loyalists from out of our midst!"

How that first night after they'd taken the Wetherburns' horse he had gotten the idea to swim away to escape, since no one else could ever catch him in the water—and how he had accidentally run into Thomas at the Chinese Bridge and how Ulysses had cut his hand trying to get control of the horse who was as headstrong as its mistress.

How well everything had gone . . . until Isaiah Chowning's horse had gotten away, they thought, and appeared safe in her stable the next morning.

How they had decided to take the Hutchinsons' horse because Sam knew he could control Burgess.

And how Thomas had come to his room that day, looking so heartbroken because Sam had let him down.

When he was finished, there was a silence as loud as any cannon being shot on the Palace Green. Sam sat staring at his hands, his head hanging. Thomas had never seen him look helpless before, and he wished that somehow it would all suddenly not be true.

"You've let us all down," Papa said finally. "Your mother, me, certainly your brother. This community—everything we Patriots stand for." His voice cracked. "Even God Himself."

Sam bit his lip and nodded. "That's why I came to you, Father. When I saw that my little brother is closer to being the kind of man you expect all your sons to be than I am, I couldn't keep it from you."

"You did the right thing by coming."

Mama patted her eyes with her handkerchief. Thomas closed his and sighed. *It's going to be all right*, he thought. Papa has forgiven him, and he'll make it right with Xavier Wormeley, and Alexander and Robert will be free. The world that had looked so hopeless a few minutes before was not so dark anymore.

And then Papa said, "What are you going to do now, Samuel?"

Sam's face went blank. "What do you mean, sir?"

"A man and his son are in the jail, accused of horse theft. That's a hanging error. You are responsible for that. What are you going to do?"

Sam's blue eyes darted to his mother and back to his father. "I thought, sir, that you would—"

"That I would *what?*" John Hutchinson said, The Look carved painfully into his face. "You thought that I would go to Xavier Wormeley and explain that your 'boyish prank' was at the bottom of all this? That I would tell him I would take my own action with you and he need not concern himself further? That I would set things right for you?"

Sam didn't say anything. His face said it all for him.

Papa burned his eyes into Sam's. "You thought that I was wrong and you were right, and so you took matters into your own hands. Continue to do so. What do you think is right in this case?"

For a moment, Sam looked to Thomas as if he were going to fly from the room, possibly through the window, in a panic. His blue eyes grew wild, and he gripped the arms of the Windsor chair until his knuckles turned white.

But Papa didn't rescue him. He only waited, while Thomas squirmed and Mama sat white-faced. And as they watched, the fear flickered in Sam's eyes . . . and then went out. He took a deep breath and straightened his big Hutchinson shoulders and set his square Hutchinson jaw.

"I must go to Xavier Wormeley myself and tell him," Sam said. "The rest is up to him."

Mama whimpered and looked at Papa with pleading eyes. But Papa nodded.

No! Thomas wanted to cry out. *He'll hang him! Xavier Wormeley will string Sam up!*

"The Lord is with you, Samuel," John Hutchinson said. "You have nothing to fear."

Sam stood up and held his blond head high. "All right, then," he said. And he was gone.

Thomas stared at the empty doorway as if by looking at it, he could make Sam come back. Virginia Hutchinson held her handkerchief to her mouth and rushed from the room in a tearful flurry of last year's satin.

Thomas bolted from his chair to follow her.

"Do all my sons distrust my judgment so?" said Papa.

Thomas stopped in midstep, held by his father's words as if he'd been pulled back by the arm. His father was standing with his back to him, gazing through the slats of the blinds out onto the Palace Green. The shafts of sunlight cast a shadow of his great shoulders in broken lines on the floor.

Suddenly, he turned and said, "Will you walk with me, Thomas?"

Thomas didn't ask where or why, and he didn't even wonder. His heart, which had been pounding so hard in anger, had all but stopped.

Papa didn't speak again until they had left the glaring sunlight behind and stepped into the cool quietness of Bruton Parish Church. He led the way to the altar and pointed to the tablets on the back wall.

"I told you once, Thomas, that God's rules are the ones we must follow. There they are, all we ever need to live by." His deep eyes flashed. "Yet when I make decisions in accord with these very laws, my sons say, 'No, Father, you're wrong! Let me do it my own way!'"

Papa heaved a deep sigh and continued. "I have Clayton, who wants to risk his life going to England, and Sam, who wants to go to war when he is still a brainless child with no skill or wisdom yet for battle. I tell them that God says they must honor their father and mother . . . and they begin their own wars!" He turned his head slowly to look at Thomas.

Disappointed lines had gathered around his mouth. "And now I have you, Thomas. You want to run away in anger when I tell you that Samuel will never learn that he must be responsible as well as charming and strong and willful, if he does not go to God and to the law himself when he breaks the rules." Papa stopped and smiled sadly. "I have begun to preach a sermon, Thomas. I mean only to tell you, I study these laws every day of my life. And I pray to the Lord for help to follow them. That is why it causes me such pain when you shake your heads and cry 'no!'"

Papa shook his own head slowly. "God doesn't change. Neither can I. Even if it means my own sons turn against me."

Thomas stared at the tablets, but he couldn't see the words written on them. His eyes were too filmy with tears.

"I won't turn against you, Papa," he said. He could feel the tears spilling over. "And I'm glad you're building ships instead of going off to the war! And I know Sam has to take his punishment—but I don't want him to hang, Papa. You won't let them hang him, will you?"

His father smothered Thomas's shoulder with his hand. "He will not hang, son, I assure you. Your brother was right— you are very close to being the man I have always hoped my sons would be." He gave the shoulder a squeeze. "You still have that fire in you, but I see that you are using it differently now. You won't always be popular for following the rules, but there will always be One on your side." Then he closed his eyes and bowed his head.

In the long moment that followed, Thomas knew his father was praying—to the One. Thomas watched him, watched his lips move, watched the sadness and the disappointment in every line in his face. There were a lot of new lines now.

Thomas closed his own eyes and began to pray. *Thank You for the rules, God. Please help me to never, never use them to put that disappointment on my father's face.*

Or Yours.

Amen.

✝ ✝ ✝

"Your father," said Esther as she pulled another pie out of the big brick oven and mopped the sweat from her forehead with her apron, "is the only person I know who would insist on having a banquet in August! He'll think twice about it if I die of heat exhaustion here in this kitchen."

Thomas added the peach pie to the sponge cake and the strawberry tarts on the table and shook his head.

"It isn't a banquet, Esther," he said. "It's just a dinner party for our friends."

"Every friend you ever had!" She dropped the apron and began counting off on her fingers. "Nicholas Quincy. Francis Pickering. Robert and Betsy Taylor—and Alexander and Caroline. Not to mention you, your father, your mother, Sam, Clayton. . . ."

"And Malcolm."

Esther sniffed. "I've been in John Hutchinson's service all my life, and I never got invited to a dinner party."

"You'll be there, Esther," Thomas said with a grin. "Every chance you get!" He looked around the kitchen. "Have I done everything? You have wood, water—"

"Yes, now scat," she said, shooing him toward the door. "It's time you got dressed. Your mama has your clothes all laid out for you."

Normally, Thomas would have groaned as he envisioned the red brocade or the lavender silk sprawled across his bed. But not this time. This night was special, and nothing could spoil it.

He was just plastering back the last stubborn corkscrew of hair from his forehead when the guests began to arrive below. He hurried down the stairs and was at once pulled into a hug by Betsy Taylor.

"If you should ever get tired of having this young man for a son," she said to Papa, "I shall be glad to take him in."

"A kind offer, Mistress Taylor," John Hutchinson said, "but I must turn it down. Will you accept a place at my table instead?" He offered her a blue taffeta arm.

"Indeed," she said, smiling her magic smile. "I understand you have a wonderful cook."

Papa's eyebrows shot up. "Where did you hear that?" he said as he led her into the dining room.

"Are you going to escort me to dinner, Tom?" Caroline said, an impish grin on her face.

Thomas knew his face was the color of the strawberry tarts they were about to eat. Why was it, he wondered, that the redness of your face controlled whether or not you could move your mouth?

It was just that she didn't look like Caroline his playmate who beat him to the tops of trees and dared him to walk the railing of the Chinese Bridge. Standing there in her yellow silk dress with the white ruffle at the neck and her hair trailing down her back in curls, she looked more like a girl who would say . . . well, "Are you going to escort me to dinner?"

"Well, are you?" she said, tossing the shimmery curls.

"He'll be fightin' me for the honor, lassie."

Malcolm strode toward them from the back hall, and Thomas stared even harder at him than he had at Caroline. Malcolm was wearing a pale-green coat and matching breeches with a cream-colored, lace-sleeved shirt and snowy-white stockings.

That's Alexander's suit! Thomas thought as he continued to stare. *He wore it the first time I ever met him!*

He looked quite different in it than Alexander, of course. Malcolm was much more rugged and brooding than the sunny teacher. But still, Thomas thought, Malcolm did look the gentleman. Even his hair was—

"Who cut your hair?" he whispered to Malcolm over Caroline's head.

"Your mother," he whispered back.

Thomas checked to see if Caroline had heard. But it appeared that she was in a trance. She was gazing at Malcolm, eyes round and brown and sweet as mince tarts.

He does look different. I even feel different, Thomas thought. *This has been a magical summer. Maybe we really are different people than we were before.*

"How handsome you are," Caroline said softly to Malcolm.

Thomas looked at her sharply. She was still gazing. Thomas's neck prickled, but not with anger. He just felt like he wanted to say to her—

"If Thomas is goin' to stand there with his mouth hangin'

open like a fly trap," Malcolm said, "then I'll escort you in myself."

Not to be outdone, Thomas stuck out an awkward arm. "We'll both do it," he said.

Giggling, Caroline took an arm on each side, and they made their way toward the dining room, while the adults nudged each other and smothered their smiles.

Say it! Thomas commanded himself firmly. *And get rid of these prickles.*

"Caroline," he whispered as they were getting into their chairs.

"What?"

Thomas wet his lips nervously. "Do you like Malcolm, um, I mean, better than you like me?"

Caroline's smile went from one pearl-dropped ear lobe to the other. "Not only are you a big, clumsy oaf," she said through a tiny hole she made out of the side of her mouth, "you're also a silly one. Of course not!" She poked him with her elbow. "You're my best friend. You always will be."

Thomas grinned and sat down and sent a fork clattering to the floor.

When they were all seated around the mahogany table, which gleamed with candles and silver and Mama's best china, Papa asked the blessing and thanked God for each person seated there.

When he got to Clayton, his voice grew a little cooler as he thanked God for Clayton's good work on the plantation, carrying on business according to Papa's wishes. Thomas sneaked a peek around the table. No one else seemed to notice it. Thomas sighed. That was one problem that hadn't been solved this summer.

When Papa got to Sam, he didn't thank God that Xavier had dismissed Sam's case because his thefts had been for the Patriot cause and Sam had always intended to return the horses to their owners. Sam had already gone to the Taylors and begged their forgiveness. There was no need to bring it up again, Papa had told all the Hutchinsons.

Robert Taylor must have told his family the same thing, Thomas thought. Alexander was being polite to Sam, and Mr. Taylor hadn't brought his pistol.

Besides, there were plenty of happier things to talk about. As Papa expertly carved a roast goose and everyone filled their plates with steaming vegetables, pigeon pie, and batter bread, the conversation flitted from one merry topic to another.

Thomas, Alexander said, would soon be ready to take his entrance exam for the Grammar School at William and Mary.

Nicholas, Francis said, was being praised as the finest doctor Williamsburg had ever seen. Clayton added that Nicholas had promised to see what he could do for his weak heart.

John Hutchinson, Robert Taylor said, had agreed to guarantee to the city his promise not to take arms against the revolution, which meant that by law he could remain in Williamsburg with his family.

Malcolm, Nicholas said, was good as new and could ride a horse again any time he wanted.

They were all cheering that news when Clayton tapped his goblet with his spoon and looked around expectantly.

"I have the most important news of all, just reported in Yorktown this morning," he said. His narrow face wore a rare smile. "Five thousand French troops under the command of a man named Rochambeau have arrived in Newport, Rhode Island, to help General Washington and the Continental Army. This could very well turn the tide of the war!"

"It will have to," Sam said. "You all know about the disaster in Camden, South Carolina. That idiot General Gates wouldn't believe that most of his men weren't battle-tested. He took them to Camden on a *night* march, and the British surprised them at two o'clock in the morning. What the wretched British didn't kill, they took as prisoners—plus all the wagons and supplies." Sam's face suddenly glowed. "The only piece of good news is that that Swamp Fighter Francis Marion and his little band of 17 men attacked a bunch of British and Tories who were taking American prisoners to Charleston—and set them all free! Serves the British right!"

"Samuel, please!" Mama said. She glanced anxiously at Betsy Taylor. "Remember our guests."

"Not to worry, Mistress Hutchinson," Robert Taylor said. "It is difficult to remember that we are enemies, eh?"

Everyone laughed nervously. Thomas looked at Caroline, who nudged him good-naturedly with her elbow.

"To think," Robert went on, "that a set of people who six years ago were doing everything they could for the mutual assistance of each other should now be cutting the throats of each other and destroying their property whenever they have an opportunity." He raised his glass. "I am thankful to God that the Hutchinsons and the Taylors bear no such malice toward each other."

Thomas wasn't sure what malice was. He'd have to ask Alexander tomorrow. But he raised his glass anyway—and spooned another helping of pigeon pie onto his plate.

"Everything is delicious, Mistress Hutchinson," Alexander said to Mama.

"It is," Papa said. He chewed with a bewildered look on his face. "What happened?"

"Why nothing, dear," Mama said, smiling across the table at Betsy Taylor.

"What did happen?" Thomas whispered to Caroline.

"Your mother borrowed our cook and sent Esther off to the market," she whispered back.

Thomas scraped more pigeon pie onto his plate.

His stomach was bulging by the time the dessert had been cleared away and the adults had adjourned to the parlor for after-dinner coffee. The parlor doors closed out Malcolm, Caroline, and Thomas.

"Palace Gardens?" Malcolm said.

Caroline and Thomas both nodded.

"I'd challenge you to a race, but I know you're not all better yet," Thomas said to Malcolm as they strolled up the Green.

"You're just afraid I'd beat you," Malcolm said.

"And you both know that I would win," said Caroline, "so what is the point in arguing?"

There's no point in arguing anything, Thomas thought as they meandered toward the Palace as carefree as the fireflies and crickets. *Malcolm is alive and we are all friends and no one had to go to jail. There is nothing else to talk about!*

"Fearsome Trio, I fear I see an obstacle ahead," Malcolm the Mighty said.

He pointed toward the Palace, and Thomas the Tireless

saw it, too. There were candles in several of the palace windows, and shadowy figures could be seen moving back and forth inside.

"Who would dare to invade our territory?" asked Caroline the Courageous, suddenly tugging at her neck ruffles as if they were getting in her way.

Malcolm crossed his arms over the celery-colored suit and wrenched his shoulders uncomfortably inside it as he narrowed his eyes at the Palace.

Thomas unbuttoned his too-tight red brocade coat and thought, *Now we don't look so different. We just look like us.* He let out a big breath. That was a relief. He didn't want them ever to change.

"I don't know," Malcolm said at last, "but it's sure we're going to find out, eh?"

He cocked an eyebrow at his partners. Caroline smiled until a thousand dimples appeared in each cheek. Thomas set his jaw and let the excitement sizzle up his backbone.

Malcolm put out his hand, and they both placed theirs on top of it. "Tomorrow we begin our quest," he said.

"What shall our plan be?" Caroline said.

Walking, Malcolm began to spin out a scheme, and Caroline wove in threads of her own as she skipped beside him. Thomas, however, was quiet as he lagged behind.

I already know what the rules are going to be, he thought. *No matter what happens in the war or even in the Palace.*

He looked up at the velvet Virginia night and smiled at God. And then he ran to catch up with the rest of the Fearsome Trio.

✠ ✤ ✠